Also by Omar El Akkad

American War

WHAT
STRANGE
PARADISE

WHAT
STRANGE
PARADISE

Omar El Akkad

Alfred A. Knopf   New York   2021

THIS IS A BORZOI BOOK
PUBLISHED BY ALFRED A. KNOPF

www.aaknopf.com

Library of Congress Cataloging-in-Publication Data
Names: El Akkad, Omar, [date] author.
Title: What strange paradise / Omar El Akkad.
Description: First edition. | New York : Alfred A. Knopf, 2021.
Identifiers: LCCN 2020021749 | ISBN 9780525657903 (hardcover) |
ISBN 9780525657910 (ebook) | ISBN 9781524712075 (open market)
Classification: LCC PS3605.L12 W48 2021 | DDC 813/.6—dc23
LC record available at https://lccn.loc.gov/2020021749

Jacket photograph by Stavros Ntagiouklas / Millennium Images, U.K.
Jacket design by Kelly Blair

Manufactured in the United States of America
First Edition

To Sonny

It did not appear to be the duty of these two men to know what was occurring at the center of the bridge; they merely blockaded the two ends of the foot planking that traversed it.

—Ambrose Bierce
An Occurrence at Owl Creek Bridge

I taught you to fight and to fly.
What more could there be?

—J. M. Barrie
Peter Pan

WHAT
STRANGE
PARADISE

Chapter One

After

The child lies on the shore. All around him the beach is littered with the wreckage of the boat and the wreckage of its passengers: shards of decking, knapsacks cleaved and gutted, bodies frozen in unnatural contortion. Dispossessed of nightfall's temporary burial, the dead ferment indecency. There's too much of spring in the day, too much light.

Facedown, with his arms outstretched, the child appears from a distance as though playing at flight. And so too in the bodies that surround him, though distended with seawater and hardening, there flicker the remnants of some silent levitation, a severance from the laws of being.

The sea is tranquil now; the storm has passed. The island, despite the debris, is calm. A pair of plump orange-necked birds, stragglers from a northbound flock, take rest on the lamppost from which hangs one end of a police cordon. In the breaks between the wailing of the sirens and the murmur of the onlookers, they can be heard singing. The species is not unique to the island nor the island to the species, but the birds, when they stop here, change the pitch of their songs. The call is an octave higher, a sharp, throat-scraping thing.

In time a crowd gathers near the site of the shipwreck, tourists and locals alike. People watch.

The eldest of them, an arthritic fisherman driven in recent years by plummeting cherubfish stocks to kitchen work at a nearby resort, says that it's never been like this before on the island. Other locals nod, because even though the history of this place is that of violent endings, of galleys flipped over the axis of their oars and fishing skiffs tangled in their own netting and once, during the war, an empty Higgins lander sheared to ribbons by shrapnel, the old man is still, in his own way, right. These are foreign dead.

No one can remember exactly when they first started washing up along the eastern coast. But in the last year it has happened with such frequency that many of the nations on whose tourists the island's economy depends have issued travel advisories. The hotels and resorts, in turn, have offered discounts. Between them, the coast guard and the morgue keep a partial count of the dead, and as of this morning it stands at 1,026 but this number is as much an abstraction as the dead themselves are to the people who live here, to whom all the shipwrecks of the previous year are a single shipwreck, all the bodies a single body.

Three officers from the municipal police force pull a long strip of caution tape along the breadth of the walkway that leads from the road to the beach. Another three wrestle with large sheets of blue boat-cover canvas, trying to build a curtain between the dead and their audience. In this way the destruction takes on an air of queer unreality, a stage play bled of movement, a fairy tale upturned.

The officers, all of them young and impatient, manage to tether the fabric to a couple of lampposts, from which the orange-necked birds whistle and flee. But even stretched to near-tearing, the canvas does little to hide the dead from view. Some of the onlookers shuffle awkwardly to the far end of the parking lot, where there's still an acute line of sight between the draping and four television news trucks. Others climb on top of parked cars and sweep their cameras across the width of the beach, some with their backs to the carnage, their own faces occupying the center of the recording. The dead become the property of the living.

Oriented as they are, many of the shipwrecked bodies appear to have been spat up landward by the sea, or of their own volition to have walked out from its depths and then collapsed a few feet later. Except the child. Relative to the others he is inverted, his head closest to the lapping waves, his feet nestled into the warmer, lighter sand that remains dry even at highest tide. He is small but somewhere along the length of his body marks the sea's farthest reach.

A wave brushes gently against the child's hair. He opens his eyes.

At first he sees nothing, his sight hampered by the sting of salt and sand and strands of his own matted hair in his eyes. His surroundings appear to him as if behind frosted glass, or on the remembering end of a dream.

But other senses awake. He hears the sound of the sea,

tame and metronomic. And beneath that, the hushed conversation of two men, inching closer to where he lies.

The child blinks the silt from his eyes; the world begins to take shape. To his left the beach curves in a long, smooth crescent until it disappears from view behind the rise of a rocky hill lined with thin, palm-like trees. It is a beautiful place, tropical and serene.

For a moment he doesn't register the dead, only their belongings: ball caps and cell phones and sticks of lip balm and forged identification cards tucked into the cheapest kind of waterproof container, tied-up party balloons. Bright-orange life vests, bloated as blisters, some wrapped around their owners, others unclaimed. A phrase book. A pair of socks.

The boy's neck is stiff and it hurts to move, but he turns slightly in the direction of the sea. In the shallows sits a rubber dinghy outfitted with police lights. Farther out, the water sheds its sandy complexion and turns a turquoise of such clarity that the tourists' sailboats seem to float atop their own shadows.

Two men approach. Baggy white containment suits cover their bodies and white gloves their hands and white masks their faces, and vaguely they remind the boy of astronauts. They move slowly around and over the bodies, occasionally nudging at them with their feet and waiting for a response. Some of the corpses they inspect wear small glittering things around their fingers or necks. The boy watches, unmoving, as the masked workers bend down and carefully pocket anything that sparkles. They speak a language he doesn't understand. They move toward him.

The boy doesn't take his eyes off them. His clothes, soaked with salt water, hold fast to his frame; he flicks his toes in the tiny puddles collected in his shoes. His jaw aches. He lifts his head from the sand. He rises.

Seeing him, one of the two workers takes off his face mask and yells. The words mean nothing to the boy but by the gesticulations he gathers that he is being ordered not to move.

The man turns, first to his colleague and then, his voice even louder now, to the officers stationed at the edge of the beach. Once alerted, they begin to sprint in the boy's direction.

The boy looks around him. To his left, past where the beach ends at a small gravel road packed with police cars and ambulances and trucks with large satellites affixed to their roofs, there stands a dense forest of the same palm-like trees that bookend the far hillside, their crowning leaflets like the skeletal remains of some many-limbed starfish, or a firework mid-burst. Everywhere else the sun shines brightly, but in the shade of the canopy there is a darkened thicket, perhaps a hiding place.

The men rush closer, yelling alien things. Pinned between the water and the land, the child turns toward the sheltering trees. He runs.

Chapter Two

Before

The highway from Homs to Damascus, spindly and unlit and lined with squat concrete barricades, was deserted but for the five buses speeding southward, past the purple-green olive groves and the terraced desert. Still, the passengers hunkered low in their seats. Some checked soccer scores on their phones and carried on quiet conversations with their seatmates, passing the time. Some rocked forward and back, trying to lull their infants to sleep, and some made the same motion though they had no children. Some slept and others fought sleep, fought what it might bring. Such were the myriad mechanics of initiation into the oldest tribe, the tribe of endless leaving.

Amir Utu sat near the back of the second bus next to his mother, Iman, his half brother, Harun, and his uncle and now stepfather, Younis. With his thumbnail he dug furiously at a wristband that misspelled his name Amin, and his age as six, not eight. Earlier, at the site of departure, the humanitarian workers said every evacuee would have to wear a wristband, but when it became clear there weren't nearly enough, they placed them only on the wrists of children, and although none of the workers could say with much confidence what purpose such a thing would serve, it turned out by chance there were exactly as many wristbands as children on the convoy, and the workers took this to be an indicator that the correct decision had been made.

Silently, Younis rubbed the edge of a coin against the passport pages on which he'd earlier pasted passable facsimiles of Egyptian visas. In the way he moved the coin against the watermarked paper, lost entirely in the task at hand, there was an air of ritual. Amir observed without emotion the man he'd only ever called, behind his back, Quiet Uncle, the man who was now responsible for Amir and his mother and this new child to whom Amir felt no connection at all. How a man so meek, who shrank back into himself so readily he seemed to wear his own skin like a too-big suit, might ever take responsibility for anyone at all, Amir couldn't imagine.

Baby Harun gummed a fold in his mother's skirt. Iman held her infant with one hand and with the other checked Amir for signs of damage. She asked him questions: "What floor did we live on? What street? The broken clock tower in the roundabout, what time did it show?"

"Leave him alone, Iman," Quiet Uncle said. "Don't keep reminding him."

But she continued. "Tell me the name of the girl you liked," she pleaded, "the one from the pastry store, the one with the French accent—do you remember? Do you remember?"

Amir stared, unable to answer. Whenever she opened her mouth his mother made a sound no different from the sound made by everything around him since the first bombs fell, a fine metallic din.

He retreated from his surroundings into the pages of a comic book. For years it had been his favorite—the adventures of a boy named Zaytoon and a girl named Zaytoona in the alleyways and fields and citadels of a city that reminded him of his own. There was no quality to the art, the shading uneven, the linework like bad stitching, the colors too bright and bleeding. But the stories had a whimsy to them. The children were adventurers, and over the course of an issue they might devise from mechanic-shop scraps a dirigible, or turn a bellows and a garden hose into a means to walk the bottom of the sea.

Amir read, captivated—not by the plot or the impossible contraptions, but by the way Zaytoon and Zaytoona's little town always seemed to reset at the beginning of every new story, as though none of the previous ones left a mark. He had never noticed this before but he noticed it now and, although he couldn't articulate it, the thing that most amazed him was the sheer *lightness* of such a repairable world. To live so lightly was the real adventure, the biggest adventure.

The buses drove onward. In peacetime the journey to Damascus might have taken an hour and a half. This time it took twenty-six.

At one of the checkpoints the passengers were marched onto the side of the road and made to stand in line and a young soldier asked them who they believed in. He phrased it this way, simply and without preamble: "Who do you believe in?" It was the fourth checkpoint of the day and at each one the evacuees had been made to wait for hours and stand outside and give plainly rehearsed answers to the same questions about their allegiance to the state and the Leader. But none had rehearsed for this, and none knew what to say to the young soldier as he marched up and down the lineup of exiles at dawn, chewing on sunflower seeds and asking, "Who do you believe in?" Some stammered and said, The government. Others said, The Leader, God bless him and his brother, and God rest his father's soul. And God bless his children, others added, our future leaders, but the soldier did not appear to approve of this answer and instantly those who'd given it wished they'd never mentioned future leaders, never mentioned a future at all. On this went, so empty the pantomime that even the young soldier himself did not seem to care when Quiet Uncle, early in line and unable to think on his feet, responded, "Whoever you want."

Years earlier, before he was disappeared, Loud Uncle said only a coward survives the absurd.

On the first day of spring the convoy reached Damascus and for a while the Utus lived as guests of a relative in a villa in the eastern district. Their host was a woman named Mona, a distant cousin on Amir's father's side of the family. Through much pleading, Quiet Uncle had persuaded her to let them stay, though it was clear that

Mona intended theirs to be a short visit, a temporary respite on the way to wherever they were going.

It was a modern-looking home of white walls aligned at right angles, a curveless cube of a style Amir had seen only in foreign magazines. Often Mona held cocktail parties in the villa's stone-tiled garden patio, beneath the scattered shade of the flowering jasmine trees, and on the mornings of these days, before any guests arrived, the Utus learned to expect a last-minute suggestion from Mona that they go visit a tourist attraction or undertake some other daylong excursion on the other side of town.

Sometimes Amir managed to avoid these trips, and if he remained out of sight and earshot for the entire evening, Mona did not seem to mind him staying home. From the confines of the servants' quarters—a tiny secondary house in the back of the garden—he would watch and listen to the voices of the guests, voices that were like his, yet alien. Dressed in fine suits and gowns that glittered under the hanging lantern lights, the attendees spoke about the success of the recent literary festival or the unacceptable surge in the price of tickets to London and Paris or about the Qatari emir's daughter buying up art at auction with her oil-field allowance and locking it away in a warehouse somewhere because of course these people have more money than taste and wasn't it just barbaric. The scent of their perfumes mingled with the scent of sizzling lamb skewers on the grill and the scent of white jasmine.

It mesmerized Amir, the revelry of their parallel world. On the outskirts of this neighborhood he had seen the shattered windows, the craters in the roads, the buildings stripped of their outsides—and so he knew the monstrous thing that had taken his father and Loud Uncle and had driven his family from their home had also, in some way, visited this place. But the men and women at this party seemed not to know or care. Late at night when the rest of his family returned from their excursion, sneaking back into the house unseen through the servants' entrance, Amir remained at his lookout watching. He stayed this way until the early hours of the morning, until the last of the guests stumbled drunk into their waiting sedans and the house grew quiet.

Often, in these hours after the festivities ended, Amir's mother ventured outside to sit in the garden and listen to the old Walkman she'd owned since childhood and had managed to save as they fled.

Sometimes Mona came out to join her. For weeks, the two had treated each other with pleasant, mechanical formality, their conversations almost entirely composed of rapid-fire greetings and well-wishes, uttered in accordance with local custom and utterly insincere.

One night, Amir peered out his bedroom window and heard Mona and his mother talking in the courtyard.

"It's a beautiful evening, isn't it?" Mona said, taking a seat on the chair next to Iman, startling her. She picked a leaf from one of the jasmine flowers nearby. "It's always beautiful this time of year. It's a blessing, really, to have weather like this."

"Yes, of course," Iman replied. "A blessing from God."

"Obviously, it's not always this way," Mona said. "Sometimes we get storms, or a cold night. But, you know, it passes."

Iman smiled and nodded. The two women sat in silence, watching the flickering lights of the old city center beyond the gates of the villa. In the garden the housemaid picked up the plates and glasses, remains of the party, and then set to wiping the soot and grease from the grill.

"Why did you come here, Iman?" Mona asked.

"I'm sorry?" Iman replied.

"Why did you leave your home? Our President says people should never turn their back on their home, and he's absolutely right. It's a terrible thing, the worst kind of crime."

"My home doesn't exist anymore, Mona," Iman said. "Our President—" She paused. "It was bombed, it was destroyed. Our whole neighborhood was destroyed."

"Don't exaggerate," Mona replied. "That's what they want you to do, the terrorists, the foreigners." She spread her arms wide. "They want you to say it's this." Then she closed her arms and held up her thumb and forefinger, an inch apart. "When you and I both know it's really this."

Iman sat up in her chair. "But you must have seen it with your own eyes," she said. "You must have seen it on television, just the other day—the rubble, the dead. You must have seen what they did to our city."

"The things they show on television?" Mona brushed her hand as though shooing away a fly. "They film those things on a soundstage abroad, they build fake sets and hire foreign actors. It's all made up."

Mona patted her houseguest's hand, a look of deep concern on her face.

"You know," she said, "you really can't let yourself be so easily fooled."

The following week, at Quiet Uncle's insistence, the Utus left Syria for good. What remained of their savings they spent buying their way aboard another brigade of buses down the length of Jordan, and then onto a huge white ferry that lumbered across the Gulf of Aqaba to Egypt. He had never spoken of the place before or shown any interest in or attachment to it, but in Egypt, Quiet Uncle said, there was at least the chance at life. He repeated this phrase, time and again: the chance at life.

In the back cabin of the ferry, Amir's mother rocked baby Harun through his crying fits while Quiet Uncle slept where he sat, the forged visa peeling off the page of his passport. Amir gazed out the window.

Loud Uncle once said none of this was real, borders being a European disease. In the flint beyond the windows there were no markers of where one territory ended and the other began—only the sea which was the sky and the sky which was the land and the land which, whomever it belonged to, was not his.

In the rear of the cabin a man sat cross-legged on the floor, reading the Quran out loud. For hours he did this, page after page, verse after verse, in a trembling, singsong cadence that rendered the whole recitation at once euphoric and funereal. And although almost all the passengers around him were visibly annoyed, none could work up the nerve to interrupt him. Amir, his head aching and the dull nothingness the bombs left in place of sounds receding, covered his ears with his hands. He could hear the world again but accented now with the faintest traces of ringing, the dying pleas of all the frequencies that from here on would be indistinguishable from silence.

When they reached the shores of Taba, its colored resort lights dancing and the music of its nightclubs faint in the distance, they were ushered off the ferry and made to wait, to be inspected. Slowly, Amir and his family moved along the rickety dockside to the customs station, the remaining wheels on the family's suitcases dragging against the floor, making a fine whistling sound as they neared the crossing. Amir watched as Quiet Uncle eyed the guards, fidgeting and fingering the page of his passport.

A young, slim customs officer with a pencil mustache waved them forward, agitated. "*Yallah, yallah,* let's go, already," he said. "We'll miss the noon prayer at this rate."

"Sorry, sir," Quiet Uncle said.

He handed four passports to the officer, who flipped to the picture pages and eyed each family member in turn.

"What kind of a name is Utu?" he said.

"I don't know, sir," Quiet Uncle replied. "I didn't choose it."

"Are you trying to be funny?"

"No, sir. Sorry."

"You're from the war?" the guard asked.

"We're not *from* the . . ." Quiet Uncle started to reply, then stopped. "Yes, sir," he said. "We have papers. Everything's approved, the ministry . . ." He gestured vaguely behind him, toward the water.

"You Muslim?" the guard asked.

"Yes, sir."

"But Shia."

Quiet Uncle shrugged and looked down.

The guard flipped through the pages of each passport, unconcerned with the visas, looking for something else, something he didn't find. He shook his head.

"You're lying," he said. "You're Jews."

Quiet Uncle looked around, hoping for some other senior officer to intervene. None did.

"How can we be Jews?" Quiet Uncle asked. "Listen, listen—do we sound like Jews?"

"You're spies," the guard said. "They train their spies to sound like your people."

"We're not," Quiet Uncle pleaded, exasperated. "I swear to God we're not."

"Prove you aren't," the guard replied, smirking.

Amir stepped forward from behind his mother, he pointed up at the guard. "Prove we are!" he shouted.

Quickly, Quiet Uncle put his hand over Amir's mouth and shoved him behind his mother. He turned back to the guard with his hands clasped together.

"He's just a little boy," he said. "He doesn't know what he's saying. Please, we've been traveling for—"

The guard cut him off. "Shut up," he said. "Act like a man."

As though nothing had happened, the guard stamped the passports and waved the family through.

"Go, go, you son of a bitch," he said, chuckling and patting Quiet Uncle on the back. "Hell, you probably are Jews."

The Utus hurried past the soldiers and through the

checkpoint, under the eye of a massive billboard on which was painted a crude portrait of a different Leader and, below that, words of congratulations on his victory in the upcoming election.

By the side of the highway they found a small phalanx of taxi and minibus drivers who made most of their money ferrying migrants from the port to the big cities. Soon they were cramped alongside a couple of other families and once again moving, the minibus rumbling down a thin dirt road past endless desert, and as the checkpoint retreated from view, Quiet Uncle ruffled Amir's hair and handed him his phone to play games on, and for the first time since the bombs fell, Amir saw his mother smile.

He believed then that it was over, that even if the place they'd crossed to was entirely unknown to him or, worse yet, entirely familiar, at least they'd survived the crossing.

Chapter Three

After

Vänna Hermes stands in the front yard of her home, raking frost and dreaming of half-eaten birds. Overnight, snow fell—only a light dusting, but still unusual for April. Sometimes the winter runs a month or two longer up in the inland mountains, the monasteries from a distance like little cotton bulbs. But it rarely snows at all anywhere else on the island.

The sun has already completed her chore. Still, Vänna pushes the rake lazily this way and that. In the early-morning quiet, broken only by the occasional wail of a passing ambulance or police car headed in the direction of the nearby beach, the rhythmic scratch of metal on grass is a soothing sound.

She sees no point in going back inside. She knows her mother will simply find some other chore to occupy what she calls cheaters' days—those mornings when overnight storms or road-shuttering accidents or the memorial of the saints and prophets compel the schools to close. It seems to Vänna that, far from serving any practical purpose, or even as tools of punishment, the chores her mother tasks her with are instead designed simply to eat up time. She wonders what her mother secretly believes she will do if not chained to these menial labors, what kind of trouble she can possibly get into. In a way, it shames her to think she can't dream up any misadventure terrible enough to contend with whatever it is that must swirl in her mother's imagination. The island reeks of smallness on days like this.

She is fifteen and fifteen feels empty, an absence of an age. Some part of her is becoming a stranger to the rest. The first time she sensed it was a year earlier, while wandering among the rocks by the sea at the foot of the sleepgum forest—the first time she'd seen the severed wings. They sat there in the soil, the bones small and L-shaped at the site of the breaking, dollops of blood like rusted coins on the feathers. Seeing them this way, severed of body, she recoiled. But a small part of her responded with something like intrigue, a fascination with the kind of creature that eats the birds but leaves the wings behind.

She envisions it as something reptilian, barbed with scales and green the color of harborberry groves, glacial until it comes time to pounce. Against the oceanside rocks its claws make a sound like a radio between stations. In the quietest hours it clambers shoreside and waits for the sunhead swifts to swoop down, a blanket of black wings descending. And at the bottomward apex, the lowest the birds will dip, it springs upward, ravenous. It leaves in the wake of its feeding the discarded appendages strewn along the forest floor. No other carrion, no sign of fight, only black-feathered wings.

It is a nightmare thing but still, in her mind, preferable to any alternative—incurable disease, unbreathable air, a new ordering of the physical world under which the swifts can no longer survive. At least in this imagining, the birds die but some other animal feeds.

Now it is spring again and near one of the hills that overlook the sea the sunhead swifts are starting to reappear. Up close their telltale feature is a small patch of orange along the neck, but at a distance they are simply a black and partway-shredded mass. In both northward and southward migration they move in waves, and for as long as Vänna can remember, the birds mark their arrival to the island with symmetrical breakings of pattern, making of themselves a shifting Rorschach test against the sky. In perfect time as they come up over the shoreline, half the flock will swing left and up, the other right and down, like a paper torn down the middle. They move this way and, as they do, they sound a cry like the high register of a harmonica, a piercing communal. For as long as Vänna can remember this is how the islanders have known to mark the changing of seasons, another winter ended.

When she was younger she used to walk out to the beachside cliffs to watch them, to transcribe the secret script of their flight paths. She kept notebooks of these tracings, and made herself believe there was a language there, a meaning to the curls and curves the birds made in the sky. But even if there wasn't, she enjoyed it, the simple act of watching the sunheads and letting the watching work its way through her hand and onto the page. There was a freedom in it, a temporary dispersal of the mundane.

But as she watches them flying up over the eastern cliffs this morning, they break into strange new formations, asymmetrical and chaotic. All but a handful turn in one direction, a trickle dissents, and then a fault line runs jagged through the heart of the flock like a landmass coming undone. Something about the island is changing, she thinks, and the birds are first to feel it.

She hears men yelling. The sound comes from across the road, somewhere within the forest of sleep-gum trees. Vänna turns away from the birds overhead; she watches the forest. Out from the mass of bronze-scaled trunks, haggard and panting, a small boy appears.

He is dressed in a T-shirt and a pair of shorts that might have once been green, but are now almost translucent, the way clothes deteriorate after many washings. He emerges from behind the trees, a thin gold chain hanging around his neck, a smear of sand on his face. Breathing hard, he stands at the edge of the road. The boy and the girl see each other, and for a moment neither one moves.

The men's voices grow louder, their source the same thicket from which the boy has just emerged. They are disjointed, irritable, one asking another, "Which way, which way?" Someone curses, and someone else says, "It's not my problem, it's your problem."

Vänna turns back to the boy, who remains in place,

wide-eyed, helpless, and although she can make no sense of him, the way his face contorts in fear as the sound of yelling grows closer suddenly renders it grotesque to simply watch him, to watch whatever comes next, and do nothing.

She calls for him to come over, but he either can't understand or is unable to hear. Instead of raising her voice, she beckons him with her hand to approach. He pauses for a moment and then, jolted by the voices pursuing him, runs across the road.

She meets the boy at the edge of the yard, where she helps him over the remains of a low stone fence that separates the Hermes property from the road. Up close she sees that he is perhaps eight or nine years old. His curly black hair is stiff with saltwater residue on the left side of his head but matted down on the right, half his face dirty with wet, clumped sand. Otherwise he looks like any other student at Vänna's school.

"What's going on?" she asks, but the boy only stares at her, uncomprehending.

She sees the sleep-gum leaves rustling up the road, the men exiting the forest a little farther north than the place from where the boy has come. She recognizes them instantly by their uniforms, and on the heels of this recognition comes another—the boy is not from the island, cannot be from the island.

"Go, go inside," she tells him, taking him by the arm and ushering him into an unused farmhouse that sits at the edge of the Hermes property. Quickly she guides him to the very back, beyond stacks of fertilizer and empty harvest crates and keepsakes from the farmhouse's once-intended use as a storage shed for her grandparents' failed bed-and-breakfast.

"Wait here," she says. The boy does not reply. Vänna moves both hands downward as though stuffing an invisible suitcase. "Sit, wait."

She leaves him there and walks outside. She stands by the old stone wall and watches as four men—two of them rookie coast guard recruits, recently graduated from Vänna's high school—search the nearby field. They are frantic, still yelling at one another, assigning and deflecting blame.

One of the men sees her. For a few seconds neither speaks, and then Vänna calmly points northward. The man nods. The search party turns away from the Hermes house and heads north.

Chapter Four

Before

N

o problem, no problem. Two for twenty franc. Okay, good price."

"*Un,* un. *Seulement.*"

"*Oui, oui,* no problem. *Deux* for twenty franc, best price."

At the foot of Pompey's Pillar a boy about Amir's age hawked T-shirts commemorating the revolution. He kept them piled on three chicken crates, next to garlands of jasmine and little packs of Kleenex and miniature Egyptian flags, a small and mobile storefront. Earlier in the day the police had chased the hawker from the boardwalk and then the road by the Hilton, and now he was here, hustling tourists.

Amir sat on the concrete blocks that fenced the ruins, watching the boy work. He was a born salesman, charming and fluent in the salutations and small talk of at least a dozen languages. He held up two shirts, letting them unfold to show the English text—JANUARY 25—REVOLUTION—TAHRIR circling an Egyptian flag. He thrust one of the shirts at the chest of a large

French tourist as though giving it away, goading him to take it. The tourist shoved it back.

"*Un, un,*" he wheezed, holding up his index finger as his wife urged him to just take both shirts and be done with it. "One. You understand."

The boy adjusted his knock-off Atlanta baseball cap. "*Oui,* yes. One, two. Two for twenty franc. Best price."

"Not two!" the French tourist yelled, reddening. He yanked both shirts from the boy's hands and threw one of them on the ground. "Only one! *Imbécile!*"

The smile never left the boy's face. "No problem," he said. "One shirt for twenty franc. Best price."

Amir watched the boy with admiration. He imagined him as a new friend; he imagined helping, in some way—carrying the chicken crates, counting the take at the end of the day. In this new country he felt a great distance from almost all the children he'd met, such that he could think of friendship only as a thing that depended on him being useful. But he couldn't bring himself to approach the boy.

At the other end of the street, not far from the gates to the ancient ruins, a couple of food trucks catered to a long lineup of tourists and locals. The tourists were mainly European, the locals upper-class, their Mercedes sedans parked haphazardly on the road and up on the sidewalks. Near one of the trucks a cook charred lamb over an open flame and in the other truck, with assembly-line efficiency, three men moved meat and cheese pies out of the oven and onto the rack, then off the rack and onto the plates. The smell of fresh-baked bread and grilled meat and za'atar rose, momentarily, over the smell of exhaust.

Amir marveled at the movement of the cooks and the movement of their customers—the simultaneous ease and frenzy with which men and women shouted orders at the truck, the way the cooks silently absorbed these orders. It amazed him, how much chaos people can put up with, so long as what needs doing gets done.

About thirty feet from the food truck, beneath the shadow of the concrete blocks, a fully veiled woman and her daughter sat on the ground, begging for change. Like the boy at the other end of the street, the woman spoke a smattering of many different languages. She gauged, quickly, the nationalities of the tourists as they walked past, and at each she hurled a plea for help. Taking their cue from the locals, the tourists ignored her.

Amir turned to look at the woman and her daughter. The girl was about five or six, barefoot and dressed in pajamas. She sat cross-legged, counting her fingers, singing a song.

Cautiously Amir hopped off the concrete barrier and walked toward the food truck. In the bustling crowd he became for a moment invisible, and none of the men inside the truck gave much notice to him as he walked around the back. Peering over the generator, he saw the counter on which the thin, freshly made pies lay, stacked in little towers. One man slid pies on, another took them off, each working in such serene, repetitive motion they became hypnotic.

For a few seconds, both cooks turned away, and before

they turned back, both Amir and a pie were gone, invisible once more in the crowd. High on adrenaline and the thrill of having gotten away with it, the prize warm in his hand, Amir ran to the place where the woman and her daughter sat.

"Here," he said, handing the pie to the woman. She refused to take it.

"Did you pay for this?" she asked. Her daughter looked up, eyeing Amir.

"Just take it," Amir said, looking back over his shoulder at the truck. One of the men was re-counting a stack of pies.

"Why would you do that?" the woman said. "Don't you understand? You've given them an excuse."

One of the cooks had eyes on them now. He opened the truck door and stepped outside.

Suddenly aware of what was about to happen, Amir flung the pie in the woman's lap and clambered over the concrete partition. Without looking back, he ran for home.

He returned to find Quiet Uncle back early from the public library, where he'd recently found work as a janitor. He sat by the window, watching the city and checking his phone every few minutes. Outside, Alexandria buzzed, preparing to celebrate the Prophet's birthday. Inside, Fairuz's voice flooded from the tape-deck speakers, which rendered the songs crackled and distorted, but still could not take away from the voice itself, its plain magic, its dueling lightness and weight. So often had Amir's mother, father and uncles played the same tape that for the first few years after Amir became cognizant of music, he believed this woman to be the only person in the world capable of making such sound, and as a result was never nearly as astounded by the beauty of music as the fact that only one person possessed the singing.

Someone in the apartment above them stomped against the thin floorboards. Quiet Uncle cursed and turned the cassette player down.

"I swear to God, that dinosaur spends the whole day with her head against the floor," he said.

"Don't let it get to you," Iman replied. Amir smelled the char of old crumbs as the kitchen element heated; soon his mother came back from the kitchen with a small cup of coffee. She set it on the table by Quiet Uncle, the liquid in the cup barely moving, thick as tar, then she returned to the kitchen to make dinner.

"They think there's only so much living to go around," Quiet Uncle said to no one, his eye on the city and through the city, through a tiny sliver of sight between the buildings, the sea.

"Sorry, what was that?" Amir's mother asked.

"Nothing," Quiet Uncle replied. "What did you buy?"

"Just a few things," Iman said. "Tomatoes, fava beans, bread. Come, sit on the couch, take your shoes off. I'll make you something to eat."

Quiet Uncle waved her away. "I'm fine. Go feed Harun."

Amir turned on the television and sat on the couch in the living room. It was a small apartment furnished with ancient chairs and couches and beds that all bore the same gaudy, faux-gold overlay. A Turkish rug, its geometric patterns long ago faded into a uniform and clayish red, lined the entryway. A cheap thrift-store painting of a tropical beach hung on the wall.

Reception depended on the clouds, and whatever the soot-lacquered pigeons on the rooftop were doing to the antennae. Sometimes a fuzzy BBC or CNN signal survived, but tonight the sole channel that came through on the sputtering cathode-ray television was local and government-run. It carried footage of a press conference.

An old man in an ill-fitting military uniform stood at a podium, talking about a cure for all diseases. He praised the ingenuity of the Egyptian military for devising an end to illness, and added that although he could not yet show the new invention to the public, it would soon mark another glorious chapter in the country's already glorious history. When he was done speaking, all the reporters in the room applauded and the man turned to the camera and saluted and the station cut to footage of the sun rising over the Nile, accompanied by a children's chorus.

"Turn off that nonsense," said Quiet Uncle from his chair by the window.

Amir's mother returned to the living room and set a bowl of beans and three rounds of thick flatbread on the table. Quiet Uncle remained in his chair, checking his phone.

"Is David still coming by tomorrow?" Iman asked.

"Who knows with these people?" Quiet Uncle replied. "It doesn't matter, anyway."

"Don't be like that," Iman replied. "It does matter. It will."

So often did his mother and Quiet Uncle mention the name of David that Amir had recently come to think of him as an apparition of sorts, not a representative of the United Nations' refugee-resettlement arm but a figment of the family's communal imagination. Amir had never seen David, only heard others in the neighborhood talk about him as one talks about the weather—predictively and with great uncertainty. David came and went and when he came, the refugees advised one another to dress appropriately.

Quiet Uncle's phone buzzed. He looked at it for a moment and then set it down carefully on the arm of his seat. He got up and kissed Amir's mother on the forehead. He smiled.

"You're right," he said. "I'm sorry. There's no use being a fatalist. Let's eat."

It had become a game of sorts, in Amir's mind—to chart these little roller coasters of his uncle's moods, the way he could hop in and out of his myriad small depressions, his waning and waxing expectations of the world.

Once, not long after they'd first arrived in Alexandria, Amir heard an argument in the other room between his mother and Quiet Uncle.

"I stepped in, didn't I?" Quiet Uncle said. "I did the right thing, after he left."

"He didn't leave," Iman replied. "He was taken."

"And that's my fault? I did something to make that happen?"

"No, you did nothing."

That ended the argument, and brought about another two days of silence.

But it wasn't even during Quiet Uncle's drawn-out sulking episodes that Amir disliked him most. It was afterward, when suddenly and with no explanation he cheered up, pretended nothing had happened; when he came back from work with a bouquet of flowers for Amir's mother, or offered to take Amir to that part of the shoreline where the manicured, palm-lined hotel beach crossed over to the littered public one but the security guards never chased the locals away. It was when he showed how easily kindness could come to him, if he wanted it to.

Evening set. Soon baby Harun was asleep in his crib and Quiet Uncle asleep in his chair, and Amir sat watching his mother watch soap operas.

They bled one into the next, their plots trite and cautious and interchangeable. The brief, chaotic life of the revolution was over and with it the interlude during which it was acceptable to speak culture to power, to craft art out of dangerous things. Recycled again now were the same stories of doomed lovers and strained familial relations between wise elders and their headstrong, naïve children, all punctuated by long, patriotic soliloquies. In this way, though the accents were different and the geography different, this new place reminded Amir of home.

He knew the reason his mother watched these shows had nothing to do with the storylines. Instead she focused on mouthing and reciting the actors' words, bending and flattening the vowels just so. And he knew the accents of the actors sounded common and vulgar to her, but if she ever hoped to avoid the immigrants' markup, every last trace of home in her voice had to be wiped clean. She needed to sound like the place in which she hoped to restart her life.

Sometimes when Amir listened to his mother talk with the other women who lived nearby, women who had fled from the same place she had, he heard them say that what really mattered were other things: the color of one's skin, the country of one's birth, the size of one's inheritance. But his mother always argued that what mattered most was to speak in a way that mimicked the majority tongue, to sound exactly like them. And even if those other things mattered more, this was all she could change.

Amir sat silently, listening to his mother snap her tongue up toward the roof of her mouth, trying for a harder-sounding *g*, a deeper-sounding *h*. In moments such as these it was difficult to think of her as a single person, the same person he'd known all his life. When she was with her friends she was someone named Iman and when she haggled with the vendors at the market she was someone named Umm Amir and when she pleaded with the British man whose position seemed to entail passing judgment on whether she and her family were sufficiently destitute to be called refugees she was Mrs. Utu, and all of these people seemed to be entirely different and engaged in entirely different attempts at survival.

The sound of a clanging bell came in through the broken window shutters. Quiet Uncle stirred in his sleep. Likely it was a trolley, or a vendor's cart; in Alexandria all sounds, like the air, had a maritime quality—something tidal, an endless circling of arrival and departure and the brief, weightless intermission of life between them.

It was Quiet Uncle who had wanted to settle here. At first Amir's mother resisted; there was a smaller migrant community in Alexandria than in Cairo, fewer jobs to be had, less room to carve out a small parcel of anonymous existence. She had wanted to stay in the capital but after a few months there, Quiet Uncle had demanded that they move to the coast. He never explained why, always said something vague about room to breathe.

A year had passed since they'd settled in Alexandria. It was a place sick with the ruins of colonial beauty. The new condominiums stood on the graves of the classic British and French and Italian villas, which stood on the graves of the Mamluk palaces, which stood on the graves of the Ottoman mosques, which stood on the graves of the Greek and Roman temples, which stood on the graves of myriad nameless and ancient villages long ago swallowed by the sea. Everywhere these identities warred and the warring produced no victorious identity, no identity at all, only the sense of manifold incompleteness, the universal aftertaste of conquest.

Still, it had the water. It had that air scrubbed clean with salt, floating over the curve of the boulevards and hanging in the light of the teardrop lampposts. It was a comforting thing, to look out at the sea, to breathe its air.

On television an old man told a young one that in the afterlife we will all meet the Prophet and to Him unburden every one of our sins and secrets. In time Amir tired of watching his mother mimic the accents of the soap-opera stars. He inched over to where Quiet Uncle sat asleep in his chair. He took his uncle's phone off the handrest to play a game on it, and when he pushed the button and the screen lit up, he saw the last message his uncle had received. It was from an unknown number and contained a single word: TONIGHT.

Chapter Five

After

The soldiers run up the road. Vänna waits until the men disappear behind a curve and then waits awhile longer. When she is certain they're gone, she returns to the farmhouse where she'd set the boy to hide.

It is a sturdy, ugly thing, made of stone and concrete washed white like the other home on the property and roofed with terra-cotta tiles. Inside the gut of the farmhouse is a single open space, above it a half hayloft, reachable by a wooden staircase. It was made to house animals, Vänna guessed. But all anyone used it for now was storage.

The plan, as Vänna understood it, was to start with a single room and build up from there. This is how her mother's parents, Linnea and Levi Olsson, settled on this property when they moved to the island as new retirees a decade before Vänna was born. They plotted it down to the penny on a spreadsheet: For the first year they'd rent out the spare bedroom in the big house, only to friends from the mainland, or people those friends vouched for. Then, when they got the hang of it, when business picked up and word got around, they'd refurbish the farmhouse, turn it into a stand-alone vacation rental. And when things started rolling, they'd buy up the barren harborberry grove next door, clear out the gnarled roots and burrow holes, and really start building.

To the best of Vänna's knowledge, only six guests ever stayed at the Baldur Inn before the business went bust. Barely a month into the first high season, the mortgage crisis that hobbled the mainland found its way to the island; tourism dried up, the big hotel and time-share constructions along the eastern shore went into hiatus. On television there was talk of belts that needed tightening and entitlements that had become, quite simply, incompatible with a modern competitive economy. She remembers those years clearly, though it was almost half her life ago—the years when the whole world seemed to go broke all at once. She remembers the sight of men and women baking in summertime heat, waiting on the banks to open, waiting on day-labor work. Ever since then she has come to associate poverty with interminable waiting. These were the waiting years, and in time the family gave up on ever reviving the Baldur Inn.

Vänna enters the farmhouse to find the boy at the far corner, peering into a brown, jug-like container. It's a jar of maple syrup, a gift from a Canadian couple who stayed at the inn many years earlier. The boy has popped the lid and chipped away at the amber crystals lining the container's neck. He eats the chippings, the hardened syrup crunching under his teeth, and as she approaches she can smell its burnt sweetness on him.

He sees her. He pauses. He backs away.

"Don't be afraid," Vänna says, but she is sure now he doesn't speak her language. He monitors her the way a small animal might monitor a rustling in the leaves.

So she too backs away. She walks to the other side of the room, where a large dismantled sign for the Baldur Inn sits alongside a few cardboard boxes full of bed linens and a cheap painting of an orange grove and the sea. She retrieves two bathroom mats from one of the boxes and places them on the ground, a couple feet apart, then sits cross-legged on one and motions for the boy to sit on the other. Never taking his eyes off her, he does.

Vänna points at herself. She says her first name. Then she turns her finger and points at the boy. He pauses for a second, as though struggling to recall it, and then, suddenly, he blurts out, "David."

Vänna nods. She points at herself again. "Vänna Hermes," she says, and points at the boy.

He seems for a moment to panic. Finally, a kind of dejection comes over him and he replies, defeated, "David Utu."

She can tell from his accent he's not of the island or even the mainland, and from his name she can divine no country of origin, nor can she figure out an easy way, using this makeshift language of pantomime, to ask him where he's come from.

So instead she points to herself again and this time holds up both hands with all ten fingers extended. Then she closes one hand into a fist and extends all five fingers on the other. Then she points at the boy.

He holds up both hands, all five fingers extended on one, four on the other.

Vänna smiles, proud of her resourcefulness, proud of prying these little doors between them open. She starts to think of something else to ask him, a way to get at the location of his family, his place of origin, how he's arrived here. But he interrupts her, cupping his right hand such that all five fingers touch. He moves his hand toward his mouth, over and over, eating air.

"Yes, of course, I'm sorry," Vänna says. "Wait here."

She gets up and leaves the boy in the farmhouse. She runs back across the lawn and the stone-tiled courtyard into her house, entering through the kitchen door.

The house is quiet. A pinewood-scented candle is doing nothing to mask the stale stink of cigarettes in the air. Vänna opens the kitchen window, then rummages through the fridge, looking for anything that might remain from a previous day's trip to the grocery store, finding nothing but condiments and a bottle of club soda. In the cupboard there's only baking powder and rat traps, a can of condensed milk and another of lemon curd, soft white fractals of mold growing inside. She begins to search the kitchen drawers, though she knows there's nothing there, when suddenly she remembers a box of shortbread cookies she bought a week earlier at a charity bake sale at school.

She turns to go to her room and finds her mother standing where the hallway meets the kitchen.

"You finished the whole yard, I suppose," she says.

"The sun finished it," Vänna replies. "It melted."

"Is that supposed to be funny?"

"Sorry," Vänna says. "Yes, I finished. I just came in to get a snack."

"You don't need a snack," her mother replies. She picks her purse off the kitchen counter and pulls out her wallet.

"Your father will be home soon," she says. "Go down to the Xenios and buy us lunch."

Vänna takes the money. Her mother lights a cigarette and turns on the tiny kitchen television.

Everyone who's ever met them has said the daughter is the spitting image of the mother. Both have the same cobalt eyes and smooth, knife-heel noses and wear their thin blond hair in a simple ponytail. Only the usual markers of age differentiate them—a few fine lines near the eyes, a little silver in the hair. Once, Vänna's mother told her she looked beautiful in the way that all people, everywhere in the world, hoped to look beautiful. They were at the beach when she said it, Vänna having just come back from building a sand castle with a couple of tourists' children, her arms and legs covered with wet sand. Her mother said it simply, without elaboration. And when she said it, she addressed Vänna but looked out at the tourists' children playing in the waves.

By turns she was a recluse, a self-imposed exile from her husband and her daughter, the only sign of her a thread of cigarette smoke blown out the bedroom window. By turns she was bitter, disappointed in something elusive, something missing from the bedrock of her life and for which Vänna couldn't help but feel responsible. Sometimes the slightest thing enraged her—the mail left out, the sheepdog let in—and when enraged she simply detached from her surroundings, went out to the back- yard to sit by the empty pool. She seemed so often a com- pendium of all her past selves, none of whom Vänna could ever interrogate, young women at various forks, turning this way or that. There were swarms of her, and Vänna did not know a single one.

On a talk show two politicians argue. There's something juvenile about the way they yell at each other, something giddy. Occasionally the station cuts from footage of the studio to show instead images of overcrowded migrant boats or men and women walking through the forest, hopping fences, dodging guards.

Vänna's mother watches, expressionless, and once more Vänna is struck by the great distance between her and this woman with whom she shares blood.

"What are you waiting for?" her mother says without turning away from the television.

"Nothing," Vänna replies. She opens the kitchen door and leaves the house.

Outside, another police car races down the road that separates the Hermes property from the sleep-gum forest and the sea. She watches it pass. On the morning news they'd said something about an accident on the beach and at first she thought it was probably some tourist. Once or twice a week, more during the high season, you could always count on some drunken foreigner falling from their cliffside balcony into the sea or getting their head slashed open in a barfight. Sometimes the tour- ists got so drunk they lost their way walking back from the beach to the Hotel Xenios—a ten-minute hike up the shoreline, if that—and they'd come wandering up the road like zombies, singing their drinking songs off-key.

They might have been her problem if things had gone differently, if the Baldur Inn had survived the recession and the austerity that followed. And she reminds herself of this whenever her mother orders her to dust the farm-house or uproot the weeds or tilt the satellite dish on the roof in the direction of some distant signal—at least she doesn't have to wait on loud, drunken foreigners. At least the inn failed.

Behind Vänna, in the side yard between the house and the remains of the long-unused harborberry grove, Dadge limps about, chasing twin ghosts—a couple of swirls of dead wildflower leaves whipped up by the wind. At fourteen, the animal is pushing antiquity, and if she was ever of any use as a sheepdog, she is useless now. Vänna watches the old dog amble, blind and deaf, sniff-ing at the two breeze-blown apparitions in the yard. She remembers the hours she'd spend as a young child chas-ing Dadge around the same yard, trying to pin a bonnet around her head.

It is a small, modest home. All over the exterior of the white stucco walls are fine lines and cracks in the paint and in the concrete, and though she often sees her par-ents argue about the cost of repairing these blemishes, what is broken in the home never looks as ugly to Vänna as the air-conditioner vents sticking out the windows, or the cables running down from the antenna and satellite dish on the roof. She likes to think that the house grows prettier as it ages. Like almost every other structure ever built on the island, she imagines the house will look prettiest in ruins.

Around the back of the home sits an unused swimming pool, empty and lined with a rough fiberglass skin. The previous owners once told Vänna's grandparents that when the house was first built, as a secluded getaway for some distant descendants of colonial nobility, the pool was laid with a bed of crushed pink coral. If that had ever been true, it certainly wasn't by the time the Olssons moved in. As the years passed and their daughter met and married Giorgos Hermes and began a new life in the old white home, and after years of putting it off, the old couple finally opened the inn only to give up on it six months later, whatever opulence lived in the house's past was confined there. Still, even though a hundred years have passed since it was made of stone and framed in the green of harborberry groves and adorned with a pool of pink coral, somehow it holds on to the memory of these things, and in this way assumes a kind of inherited dignity unique to houses, even small ones, that begin life in the ownership of the rich. Whenever Vänna's grandparents used to speak of the place, they inevitably slipped and began referring to all the grand things they were told it used to be.

It's warmer out; Vänna slips her sandals off at the start of the beach-bound road and walks barefoot down a sandy path she knows by heart. The air is sharp with salt and the wind makes of the sleep-gum leaves a murmuring crowd.

It gets this way most years, right around the middle

of April—quiet; the island, like much of the mainland, silent in preparation for the holy weekend, the tourists well dressed and on their best behavior, the big cities deserted and the small towns full. Hers has never been an observant family, but Vänna always enjoys the small awing pantomime through which her whole island passes in the days before the big Sunday ceremonies. The ceremonies themselves, with their ornate, arcane rituals and fleeting reverence, don't interest her, only the calm that comes before.

Between the beach and the Hotel Xenios rises a wide hill of dirt and brush. Where the hill drops and levels at the edge of the water, a wide footpath leads from the hotel grounds, and this is the fastest route from Vänna's house. Most days, she likes to avoid the path and instead walk up the middle of the hill, following no discernible trail. At the peak of the hill, looking north, she's able to see beyond the end of the island, beyond the fields and the ancient ruins, all the way to the lighthouse at the northeast tip, abandoned and long ago gone dark. But on this day, hurrying, she takes the footpath at the base of the hill.

She rarely spends much time by this part of the shoreline. Slowly the nearby resort has come to consume the place, as resorts and restaurants and gift shops have come to consume so much of the island's outer rim in the years since the tourist money started coming back.

The most obvious evidence of this transformation, or at least the one that annoys Vänna most, is a large party boat, decorated with strings of colored lights and per-

manently docked at the foot of the Hotel Xenios property. Most nights, it functions as a nightclub for the hotel
residents, and from her bedroom Vänna can always hear
the music. As of late, the DJ's track of choice is a rap
song whose backing music—a four-drumbeat pattern
on a tabla followed by a high-pitched, Middle Eastern–
sounding flute—Vänna despises. They play it every night,
incessantly, like a beacon.

Just before she reaches the beachfront, she sees a small
cluster of folding desks and chairs, haphazardly arranged
under a blue canvas tarp. A chaotic group of coast guard,
police and army officers buzz about the makeshift command center. The sound of satellite phones, printers and
fax machines carries over the sound of waves. On the
other side of the road, a young police officer is caught up
in a shouting match with two photographers trying to
reach over and move a tarp that blocks the beach from
view. The men wear big identification badges on lanyards
around their necks and these they wave in the officer's
face, indignant.

In the middle of the canvas-covered encampment,
Vänna recognizes one of the coast guard officers, a boy
named Ronis. He is the older brother of one of her classmates, pleasant enough if not particularly bright. She
sees him sitting at one of the folding tables, a laptop
and sheets of paper on the desk in front of him. Unnoticed, she traverses the gaggle of arguing, harried men
and walks over to him.

"What's going on?" she asks.

Ronis looks up from the sheets of paper that have until

then consumed his attention. The sheets are divided with ruler and pencil into a grid of sorts. Some of the boxes contain names, others ages, others nationalities. Most contain nothing.

"A mess," Ronis says. He points toward the beach. "I swear, you'd think they'd never seen a shipwreck before, as though we don't have one of these tissue-paper boats going under every single day."

Vänna looks out at the beach, blocked from view behind the raised tarp. She sees an ambulance slowly backing into the nearby parking lot, two police officers drawing the canvas back like theater curtains to let the vehicle through.

"What happened?" she asks.

"A migrant boat sank just off the shore. Must've come apart in last night's storm."

He shakes his head. "The bodies have been washing up on shore all day. A mess, just a mess."

Vänna pauses. She looks at the papers on the desk. "Are those their names?" she asks.

"Just a few," Ronis replies. "The ones who had identification cards, or they wrote their names on their skin and the sea didn't wash it out." He shrugs. "But even those, we don't know if they're lying. You never know with these people."

"Can you look up a name for me?" Vänna asks.

"Huh?"

"Utu. Is there anyone called Utu on the list?"

Ronis looks at his notes and then the computer screen. "I don't think so. I just got here, so I don't know. Why?"

"No reason," Vänna says. "I just saw on the news this

morning, they were talking about someone named Utu coming ashore, I think two or three days ago, but it was probably something different."

"It must have been," Ronis replies. "This just happened this morning."

He leans back in his chair and pulls a plump orange life jacket from a pile behind him. "Look at this," he says. "Look at what they were wearing. You know what's inside these things? Foam. They suck up water like a sponge."

Ronis tosses the jacket back on the pile and shakes his head.

"These people, they don't think," he says. "They don't plan."

Chapter Six

Before

Amir lay awake in bed, listening. A little after midnight, he heard footsteps in the hall.

He eased from his bed and crept to the door. He saw Quiet Uncle walking out of the bedroom down the hall, his steps light and careful, fluent in the places where the floorboards creaked. He wore plain gray pants and a simple work shirt, both recently ironed. Amir watched as his uncle typed something on his phone and then, softly easing the front door open, left the house.

Once, years earlier, Amir's father told him that none of this started with bombs or bullets or a few stupid kids spray-painting the slogans of revolution on the walls. It started with a drought. You come from farmers, he said, and five years before you were born the earth turned on us, the earth withheld. We are the products of that withholding. Every man you ever meet is nothing but the product of what was withheld from him, what he feels owed.

Don't call this a conflict, Amir's father said. There's no such thing as conflict. There's only scarcity, there's only need.

Amir looked down the hall to the other bedroom, where his mother and half brother lay sleeping. Then he followed Quiet Uncle out the front door.

A year of experience had taught Amir that Egyptians did their living exclusively at night. He stayed well back of his uncle, unnoticed among the vendors of roasted peanuts and charred corn and all the people out walking along the corniche, entire families whose respite from the drudgery of the workday was to be outside, to simply exist. Everywhere around him music played and car horns blared and conversations collided, the city overfull with living.

He followed for an hour, until Amir saw Quiet Uncle turn onto a pier at which only a single aging ferry was docked. Two old men sat at the entrance to the pier and before them a long line of people waited to board. The men appeared to be guards of a sort, talking to each person in line before letting them through or turning them away. Some of the people waved printed sheets of paper, while others showed things on their cell phone screens, and others simply offered cash. Slowly, the queue moved in the direction of the waiting vessel.

Amir inched closer. He noticed another pair of guards at the far end of the dock, younger, standing at the ramp. They wore baseball caps that partially obscured their faces, and they appeared to be checking the people in line much more closely than the two old men at the entrance. Occasionally one of the young men looked farther down to the end of the line. For a second, Amir thought he had been spotted; quickly he hid behind a table at an adjacent street café.

Four teenage boys walking down the corniche stopped in front of him to gawk at the lineup of men and women, who in appearance did not look Egyptian, but rather were a vast mixture of ethnicities and spoken languages and colors of skin. They varied just as widely by age too, from newborns to seniors, and though they all chatted as they waited to board, they spoke quietly and only to the people immediately beside them.

Some of the men and women carried small backpacks, but most carried nothing. And those who did bring luggage seemed especially meek, holding the bags close to their chests. Amir watched as a police officer walked past the assemblage, nodding at the guards and continuing on his way, unconcerned.

The four teenagers who'd stopped to see what was happening tried to start a conversation with some of the people waiting in line, but none would speak, so they turned instead to the two old men.

"Hey, Hajj, where are they going this time?" one asked.

"Mind your own business," one of the old men replied.

The teenager turned back to the people in line. "Let me guess, they told you you're going to America, right? Freedom, McDonald's, Tom Cruise, all that horseshit?"

The passengers shuffled along.

"They're going north," the old man said. "Happy now? They're sailing to Kos Town."

At the mention of the place, the four teenagers broke into hysterical laughter.

"Kos Town!" one of the boys said, struggling for breath. "Why didn't you say so? Make some room, then. I want to go to Kos Town."

"Me too," said another. "Every night I'm out here trying to get to Kos Town."

The old man bent down and removed his sandal from his left foot. He held it up high, as though readying to throw it.

"Get out of here," he said. "You hear me? Go!"

The boys walked away, still laughing. The old man turned to the people in line.

"Ignore them," he said. "They weren't raised properly."

Absorbed in this exchange, Amir did not notice that the other old man had spotted him hiding behind the tables. It wasn't until he approached that Amir saw him. In his haste to flee, he nearly knocked a glass of cane juice off a nearby table.

"Relax, relax," the man said. "What are you doing here?"

"Nothing," Amir replied.

"Don't be afraid—it's all right. You were watching that boat, weren't you?" The old man looked around. "Are your parents here?"

Amir said nothing. The man turned to face the pier, where Amir saw that one of the guards near the ramp was staring directly at them. He gave an almost imperceptible nod to the old man, who nodded back.

"How would you like to go for a trip?" he asked Amir.

"What?" Amir replied.

"But you have to keep it secret, just between you and me, all right?" The old man pointed at the assembled crowd. "All these people paid a lot of money to go on this trip. But you—I'll let you go for free. How about that?"

"Why?" Amir asked.

The old man laughed. "Because I'm feeling generous," he said. "But make up your mind quickly, before I choose someone else."

"Where's it going?" Amir asked.

"It's a sightseeing trip, the kind the tourists pay a lot of money for," the old man said. "You know what? Now that I think about it, maybe I'll just sell your spot to one of them."

"No, no," Amir said, watching his uncle board the ferry. "I want to go."

"Will you do exactly what I tell you?" the old man asked.

"Yes."

"All right, fine, I'll let you go," the old man said. He ushered Amir past most of the waiting crowd, tucking him between two people in line, just a few feet from the end of the dock.

"When you get to the ramp, you just look down and keep walking," he said. "Don't say anything."

Amir could see that the two guards were now looking in his direction, and could not possibly have missed him. But he did as the old man said and kept his head down as the line neared the ramp. He walked onto the boat unquestioned. Cautiously he stepped into the inner cabin, worried he would be spotted by his uncle, but inside he found a dense mass of bodies, against whose knees and legs he collided. Within the crowd, he became invisible.

A row of cheap plastic seats lined the far corner of the cabin, and on the ground nearby Amir found a small square of floor on which to sit. To his right, a heavily pregnant woman, veiled in a black niqab, spoke to no one in particular.

"They said how many hours?" the woman asked.

"Just two or three," another woman nearby replied. "Don't worry, it'll be fine."

"It doesn't look anything like what they had in the picture."

"The man said it's better to go on a small one like this. It doesn't attract attention like the cruise ship in the picture, and it's made of something strong—carbon fiber, fiberglass, I don't know."

The pregnant woman knocked on the side of the inner wall. "God sustains," she said. "God sustains."

She unfolded a piece of paper in her hand, on which were written English words spelled phonetically in Arabic letters. She began to practice, speaking a language she could not speak.

"Hello. I am pregnant. I will have baby on April twenty-eight. I need hospital and doctor to have safe baby. Please help."

For another hour the passengers continued boarding. Soon the compartments were so full that there was no room to sit and little left to stand, the bodies compressed against one another. Then, with a shudder and groan, the ferry eased from the dock.

Amir saw Alexandria shrink to nothingness in the background, folding into the water. His mother told him there used to be a lighthouse here, in its time one of the greatest structures ever built, until earthquakes and sabotage brought it down. He imagined it now, somewhere beneath him. He imagined it still at work, the seabed alive with circling light.

The ferry shook against the parting and unparting waves but no one seemed to mind. After a few minutes, Amir saw the two young men who'd earlier guarded the dock. They entered the lower cabin along with a few others. They carried armfuls of bright-orange life jackets. One of them also carried a manifest, and slowly they moved around the cabin, handing out the jackets to some of the passengers.

A middle-aged man dressed in a suit and tie stood and confronted them. From his accent Amir could tell he was Syrian.

"Why are you only giving them out to some of these people?" he demanded. "Why don't you have enough for all of us?"

One of the men told him to sit back down. He refused.

"Who are you giving them to?" he asked. "Who are these people, your friends? Your family? This is unfair."

"We're giving them to the ones who paid for them," the man said. He was slim, young, with a wispy mustache and a day's stubble. He wore jeans and a T-shirt marked with a small green crocodile, and though others were dressed in more formal clothing or more carefully groomed, he appeared the most arresting presence in the room, the one on whom all eyes fixed.

"We paid for passage, didn't we?" the Syrian protested. "Passage should come with life jackets. You don't sell a man a pair of shoes and withhold the laces."

"I didn't sell you a pair of shoes," the man with the manifest replied. "Sit down and shut up."

The conversation was interrupted by a slowing of the ferry. Soon it bobbed in place up and over the waves, all forward momentum gone.

"Are we here already?" the pregnant woman asked her seatmates. "Was it really that near, the whole time?"

Suddenly a blinding silver light flooded the cabin from somewhere in the darkness outside. The passengers covered their faces and tried to make out its source.

"It must be the coast guard, the police," the woman said. "I can't go back. I don't care, throw me in the ocean, I can't go back."

"Lady, what's your name?" asked one of the men who'd been passing out the life jackets.

"Umm Ibrahim," the woman replied.

"Calm down, Umm Ibrahim. It's not the coast guard, it's not the police."

The man turned and spoke to the cabin, his voice louder now.

"Everyone is going to do this exactly the way we tell you. You rush, you fight, you argue, and you can go ahead and swim."

No one responded.

"Good," he continued. "Now, all of you, sit and wait your turn."

Amir watched as the men swung open the cabin doors. On the outside deck, they seemed to shout commands into the nothingness. It was only when the spotlights swung away for a moment that Amir was able to make out the vessel at which they had been barking orders.

A decrepit fishing boat, perhaps a hundred feet in length, moved alongside the ferry, the red paint on its hull faded and flaking, the mainsail in tatters. Written in English on the side of the hull was the name of the vessel, CALYPSO.

A couple of men on the fishing boat stood portside, leaning over the gunwale. They lowered half a dozen bumpers down its side, level with the nearing ferry. Then they tossed a pair of thick, braided ropes to their partners, who grabbed them and pulled the two ships closer.

"What's going on?" the Syrian asked. "What is that piece of shit? We want to stay on this one."

The man with the manifest chuckled. "You think we're going to risk the Westerners impounding the expensive ship? Stop acting like a child. It'll make the trip just fine, and once their coast guard spots you, they'll tow you in; you won't even need an engine."

The smugglers lowered a rickety metal ramp between both vessels. Amir watched as a procession of passengers, almost without exception dark-skinned, were led across first, shivering from standing outside on the ferry's upper deck. All were ushered down to the fishing boat's lower cabin, save for two scrawny young men who were made to wait near the bulkhead.

The man with the manifest returned to the ferry's lower cabin. "Now, we'll take the ones who paid for the top deck. Don't try to be clever—we know exactly who paid for what."

The ferry began to empty, the remaining passengers exiting and crossing the ramp. It was as the last few trickled out that Amir felt a hand on his shoulder. He turned to see Quiet Uncle.

"What did you do?" he said, his voice a notch above a whisper. "How did you get on this ship?"

Amir tried to break free from his uncle's grasp. "What, I did the same thing you did," he protested. "Why do you get to take a ride and we don't?"

Something snapped in his uncle then; a viciousness took him and he grabbed Amir by the throat. It was only for a second and for the first eternity of that second it wasn't the pain of choking that shocked Amir but the fact that his uncle had such violence in him.

Then he released his grip. He dropped to his knees.

The man with the manifest, noticing the conversation, left his place at the ramp and approached the two.

"Do you know this kid?" he asked.

"What do you mean do I know him?" Quiet Uncle replied. "He's my nephew. Why did you allow him to board? He's a child all alone, for God's sake. Why would you ever let him board?"

"It's none of your business what we do," the man replied. "If he's yours, you have to pay for his ticket." The man looked at his manifest. "Younis Utu, right? You paid twenty-five hundred dollars for a place on the top deck. You have another twenty-five hundred for this kid?"

Quiet Uncle rubbed his temple. "Let me think a minute."

"Brother, there's nothing to think about," the man replied. "You do or you don't."

"Just send him back on this ferry," Quiet Uncle pleaded. "What difference does it make to you? He got on by accident."

"Nobody got on by accident," the man said. "We're happy to pay his fare if you can't, but then he's not yours anymore. He's ours, and we have a right to recoup our costs."

"Wait, wait," Quiet Uncle said. He lifted his shirt, revealing a small stack of euros and dollars taped to his stomach.

"I have another fifteen hundred," he said. "Take it."

The man shrugged. "Not enough."

"No," Quiet Uncle said. "I saw you talking to the others, I know the bottom deck costs fifteen hundred. You put me there, you put him up top."

The man furrowed his brows. "You want to go down to the bottom deck?" he asked. "Down with the Africans?"

"Brother, there are Africans on both decks," Quiet Uncle said.

The smuggler waved his hand dismissively. "You know what I mean."

Quiet Uncle nodded. "Yes, I want to go down with the Africans."

The smuggler shrugged. "It's your choice. Let's go—you'll make us late."

Quiet Uncle knelt back down to Amir. From around his neck, he removed a bell-shaped gold locket. He placed it around Amir's neck.

"Listen very carefully," he said. "We're just going on a short trip."

"I know," Amir replied. "The old man told me."

"Just listen. This trip might be a little difficult. But you just sit with everyone else and you keep quiet and it'll be over before you know it."

Quiet Uncle took his life jacket and unzipped it and helped Amir's arms through the holes. The jacket was made for an adult, and Amir struggled to keep it from riding up over his face.

"Don't be . . ." Quiet Uncle started. "Don't be difficult. Just sit. We'll be all right."

They followed the man with the manifest onto the fishing boat. By the time they boarded, every inch of the topmost deck was taken up by standing and sitting bodies.

"Push back against the railing," the man with the manifest shouted. "Make room, make room."

All around him, the other men running the operation began to strip the vessel of its electronic and illuminating tools—they dismantled the radio antennae from atop the bulkhead, unscrewed the receiver and tore down the overhead spotlights. But for the small blue glow of the passengers' cell phones, the ship went dark.

Upon seeing Amir walk onto the deck, a thin young man who sat silently among the passengers near the rear of the boat motioned with his hands to the smuggler with the manifest. He pointed at Amir and turned his hand in a questioning motion. The smuggler shook his head.

"He's paid up," he yelled across the deck. "He's not for the market."

The other man shrugged.

The smuggler flicked on a flashlight. He pointed its beam at the two men who'd been made to wait by the bulkhead.

"Eritrean?" he asked.

The men nodded.

"You speak English, Arabic, Tigre?"

The men nodded.

In a mash of all three languages, the smuggler continued.

"You know how to steer this?" he asked.

"No," the shorter of the two Eritreans replied.

"It's easy; look." The smuggler pointed the flashlight's beam to the throttle and the wheel, then to a small dashboard compass. "You see that little arrow? You make sure it stays on *N*. That's it, that's all it takes. If the arrow moves, you turn the wheel like you're driving a car, until it comes back to *N*. Come storms, come police, come military, come God Himself, I don't care. You stay in the direction of *N*. Your whole future is *N*."

He pointed the flashlight's beam back toward the ferry, and then into the darkness to the south of the boat, where somewhere in the oblivion of both distance and time lay the city from which they'd embarked, swallowed now by sea.

"And if you decide to turn around, we'll know. And then we'll come find you and we'll sink this thing and everyone on it. Do you understand?"

The men nodded.

"Good."

The smuggler ordered all the others who'd been stripping the boat to return to the ferry. As he came to follow them, the middle-aged Syrian who'd accosted him earlier stood up from the pile of old netting on which he'd been sitting.

"Is that it?" he asked. "You're getting these two who've

never been off dry land before to take us? No lights, no maps, no nothing? What kind of man are you? We'll die out here."

The smuggler crossed back onto the ferry and un-clasped the ramp behind him. "Brother, you'll die every-where," he said.

Chapter Seven

After

Amir climbs the wooden staircase to the hayloft. The thin plywood floor smells of sawdust. Through the hayloft's open window he
can see more of the island. To one side, in the far distance, there are mountains, snowcapped and sheer, to
the other are the forest and the sea, and ahead are waves
of rolling, desolate hills, scattered brush.

Below in the yard the girl walks quickly by. He watches
her head up the road toward the trees.

He has never seen a girl like her before—perhaps on
television, on the American shows, but not in the flesh.
He felt when he first saw her that she looked familiar,
but it is only now he understands why. She looks like
the illustrated girl on the canister of powdered milk his
mother buys for his baby brother. They could never afford
the good kind of anything, but his mother always made
sure to buy the expensive powdered milk. He quickly
learned you could tell the quality of a product by how
Western the people on the packaging looked. White skin,

blue eyes, blond hair—these things spoke of luxury, betterment, possibility.

The girl disappears down a side road, and Amir begins to suspect she might not come back. He thought she had understood him earlier, when he explained how hungry he was, but now he wonders if she didn't at all.

Amir puts his hand to his chest. The bell-shaped locket Quiet Uncle gave him is still there. But for a thin scratch along its exterior it has not been damaged, and the tiny portraits of his mother and brother inside are untouched.

He had been there when both pictures were taken in a small photographer's studio near their home, not long before they were forced to flee. Each family member in turn was positioned before a sheet of purple imitation velvet. The photographer worked quickly and without much interest in his subjects. The whole family had their portraits taken in less than five minutes.

There seemed then to Amir an air of futility to it all. Elsewhere their neighbors were packing suitcases, hoarding supplies, securing and, if need be, forging travel documents. And yet for some reason Amir's mother had been adamant on going to the makeshift photography studio down the street and getting these portraits taken. Amir saw no use in it, and would not respond to the photographer's request to look his way and smile.

Now, observing his mother's face inside the locket—a face that projected a kind of contentment with life as it was, a calmness—he feels that when he gets home he should apologize for having been difficult that day.

Amir closes the locket. In the afternoon heat he feels

a warmth come over him. His clothes, though starched almost crisp with the residual salt of the sea, have nonetheless dried and no longer hold fast to his skin. Earlier, after he ate a few clumps of that strange sweet stuff in the nearby pot, he felt almost fully rejuvenated. But now his stomach aches and soon he falls into a stupor. He lies down and closes his eyes. But only moments later he hears the sound of a hushed conversation, spoken in his own language from somewhere outside. He stays flat on his stomach and inches toward the window to get a better look.

A couple, in their late teens, perhaps, walk cautiously toward the fallow harborberry grove to the west. The man carries a gym bag gutted open at the zipper line, its contents exposed—a few pieces of clothing, two apples and a soda can. The woman holds her phone to the sky, waving it here and there like a divining rod. They look emaciated, journey-worn. They move with slow, deliberate steps, monitoring their periphery as they go.

They appear fearful and out of place, but Amir silently rejoices at the sight and sound of them. They speak his language; maybe they know the way home.

As he considers whether to show himself and yell down to them, Amir is startled by another sound from the vicinity of the nearby house. He peers out the window to find a woman standing at the edge of the home's stone courtyard, an old hunting rifle in her hand. She points it at the teenagers and issues a command in a language Amir can't decipher. Reflexively, they drop their luggage and raise their hands in the air.

The woman looks to Amir exactly like the blond girl

who earlier offered him sanctuary—taller and older, but clearly her kin. He watches as the teenagers plead with the woman to put down the gun, each sentence a mash of languages. But she doesn't respond except to slightly tip the barrel of the gun toward the ground a couple of times. The couple get down on their knees.

A small hatchback pulls into the driveway, coming to a stop a few feet from where the woman stands. She ignores its existence entirely, focused only on the young couple. A short, slight man gets out of the car and, taking in the scene, begins speaking in urgent tones.

The woman replies with a single word Amir is unable to understand.

The man tries to respond, but she cuts him off. She turns not just her head but, for an instant, her whole body, such that her weapon momentarily points at the man. She repeats the same word. The man nods and runs into the house. As though no conversation has taken place at all, the woman trains her gun back on the teenagers kneeling in the yard.

One of the teenagers says something in broken English and reaches into his bag, but as soon as he does, the woman at the other end of the yard fires. She aims for the space above their kneeling bodies, and the two of them fall flat to the ground as though the bullets had gone through them. In the outbuilding, Amir too pushes himself down against the plywood, the terrible reverberation of gunfire running through him, dragging with it the memory of every past reverberation.

They stay there, all of them, until, a few minutes later, a couple of trucks, painted the dark green of military cam-

ouflage, come racing up the road. The trucks pull into
the driveway and four young-looking soldiers emerge,
then a fifth man—older and more broadly built than the
others, and by demeanor their superior. The man issues
a command to the four, who reply immediately in unison and then make for the teenagers. Though there are
twice as many of them, and all armed, the four soldiers
approach with caution, spreading out and making paren-
theses of themselves around the couple, like trappers
closing on a wounded predator.

Calmly and without a hint of doubt, the commanding
officer walks to the woman holding the rifle. He moves
with an obvious limp, his left foot less like a foot than a
crutch on which the rest of him pivots. He says something to the woman and then lowers her rifle until it faces
the ground. He puts his hand on her shoulder and smiles
and it is only then that the woman seems to reemerge
from her trance. She stops looking at the young couple,
who, moments later, are bound with zip ties and taken
away by the soldiers. They board the trucks and leave
the driveway. For a while after they leave the woman just
stands there, rifle by her side, and Amir is unable to tell
from the expression on her face whether she's excited or
frightened or feels nothing at all. Then she walks back
into the house, and not long after, Amir hears the sound
of fevered shouting coming from inside, but the whole
affair ends as abruptly as it began.

He lies for a long time afterward on the plywood by
the half-open window. The edge of the hayloft is lined
with old paint cans and brushes hardened to cracking.
Whoever tried to paint the interior of the farmhouse

completed only a small patch near the ceiling. Everywhere else, the wood and the stonework shine through.

With utter confusion, he tries to make sense of the baffling play he's just witnessed, performed with such intensity by a troupe whose actors were barricaded from one another by walls of language and place and purpose, two opposing scripts come alive on one shared stage, its director absent or impotent or wholly uncaring.

Chapter Eight

Before

The *Calypso* shook and sputtered. A sound like asthmatic wheezing came from somewhere belowdecks, the scent of diesel fumes filling the air. The boat moved but in the darkness the geography of movement was indistinguishable from the geography of stillness.

A storm came. Rain fell, vaporous as steam at first, then hard and piercing. The sea, for a moment, took flight, and though in the thrashing of the waves it felt like the vessel, rickety and worn, was on the verge of sinking, it remained afloat and moving, the Eritreans struggling mightily to keep the compass arrow fixed on *N*.

Amir settled into his small cocoon of space on the topmost deck. He hugged his shins and made himself small between the feet of Umm Ibrahim, the pregnant woman next to whom he'd sat on the ferry ride to the *Calypso*. As soon as the boat collided with the seaborne storm, most of the passengers on the top deck began to panic. But Umm Ibrahim paid no attention to any of this. She simply lowered her head and, by the small light of her phone screen, commenced memorizing and reciting the words she intended to say on landfall.

Hello. I am pregnant. I will have baby on April twenty-eight. I need hospital and doctor to have safe baby. Please help.

With no one left to complain to, some of the passengers instead took their anger out on the two Eritreans who'd been drafted cocaptains. "You're already lost," one man screamed in English. "You don't know what you're doing." To which Teddy, the Eritrean more fluent in English, could only raise his arms in resignation and say, "Do you?"

Soon the storm worsened, the waves grew fiercer and the boat's vicious rocking scared the passengers back to their seats. They held on to the side of the gunwale railing, and in the dark the boat filled with the sound of pleas and prayers. Amir sank into his oversize life vest. Each wave lifted the boat high and dropped it into the preemptive crevice of the next. Feeling a sensation of the ground giving way beneath him, Amir involuntarily held on to Umm Ibrahim's swollen ankles to steady himself. He felt the woman's hands on the shoulders of his life vest, struggling to steady herself as well.

"Just sit down and don't move," said the thin man who earlier had asked one of the smugglers about Amir, an Egyptian who would only give his name as Mohamed. "The sea is like this—in a minute it'll pass."

Nobody listened, but as quickly as it started, the storm began to recede. The water calmed and the waves evened out and the rain turned once more to steam. In the dark, Amir heard some of the passengers laugh uncontrollably, a reflexive response to survival. Others applauded, though Amir could not tell who they were cheering for, and suspected that they themselves did not know. Something communal, a relief-born friendliness, now took hold among the passengers. They began to talk to one another.

A few feet across the deck from him, Amir heard a couple of men arguing. One of them stood, and a moment later Amir's small corner of the boat lit up. When his eyes readjusted, he saw the middle-aged Syrian who'd argued with the smugglers on the ferry. He stood next to a glass lantern hanging off a wooden pole that might have once served as a tiller arm. He placed a flashlight inside the lantern, and the stern of the boat lit up with shards of broken light. It did little good, but at least now Amir could see faint outlines of his neighbors, shades and silhouettes where once there was only breathing dark.

"There," the Syrian said, addressing another man, from whom he'd apparently wrestled away the flashlight. "What kind of person tries to keep light for himself?"

He returned to his seat across from Amir, a clearing in the shape of him that the others had immediately filled when he went to place the flashlight in the lantern, and which he had to elbow his way back into. He was a tired-looking man, dark circles under his eyes and a kind of shapelessness growing out from the sagging flesh of his jawline. Without knowing why, Amir immediately took him for a government bureaucrat, someone who signed papers that allowed other people to do things.

Soon the passengers began to trust that the storm had truly passed. Some took advantage of the calm to sleep, nodding off where they sat. Others, including the Syrian, struck up a conversation, introducing themselves to the people around them.

Amir did not pay attention to the conversation, until he noticed the Syrian, who introduced himself as Walid Bin Walid, talking about him.

"Look at this," Walid said, pointing at Amir. "He's wearing a vest twice as big as he is. It makes no sense. It's a vest for a man, not a boy."

"It's not too big," Amir yelled back. "You're too big!"

"Leave the boy alone," replied another man, a slim, bald Egyptian who looked to be in his late twenties and who would, during the ensuing conversation, introduce himself to the neighboring passengers as Kamal Roushdy. "Who cares if it's big for him? Maybe it'll save his life if this piece of garbage springs a leak."

"It's about more than that," Walid replied. "These men took our money. They're handing out life vests made for adults to little kids; God knows what else they're doing improperly."

At this, Mohamed started laughing.

"You're on a matchbook in the middle of the ocean and you're talking about doing things properly," he said. "Brother, you left *properly* behind on the dock."

Walid pointed at Mohamed but spoke to the people around him. "That's their man, by the way," he said. "I knew they wouldn't send us out without a spy onboard."

Mohamed nodded. "That's right," he said. "And you better believe they have people on the other side as well, people who can find you even if you make it all the way up to Sweden, America, the moon. Now keep your mouth shut so I don't have to let them know you're making trouble, and leave that boy alone."

Walid turned away. "It's not right," he said, talking to himself but staring at Amir.

The boat sailed on. At times the clouds overhead uncoupled and a wash of moonlight gave the whole vessel shape. Hours passed. Amir waited for dawn, for light.

He heard a commotion coming from mid-vessel. The Eritreans had decided to work in shifts. Teddy prepared to descend to a small crawl space at the bottom of the wheelhouse to sleep while his partner steered. But some of the passengers nearby were arguing that both should stay.

"Why do you care?" Teddy said to the passengers. "I thought you said we don't know what we're doing. We'll both collapse if we don't take turns."

"They wouldn't have told you both to do it if the work didn't require two men," one of the passengers protested.

"This work doesn't require two men," Teddy replied. He waved at the throttle, the clouded compass and the splintered wheel. "I'm not sure it even requires one."

He disappeared into the crevice at the foot of the wheelhouse, curling up with his jacket for a blanket.

Watching him, Amir thought the man was descending to the lower deck, the place where Quiet Uncle and most of the passengers were penned. He'd seen them earlier, marching downward, one of the smugglers shutting the door behind them with a padlock. Of all the chaos of the passing storm and the passengers' screams and prayers, it was the sound of people beneath the boards that frightened him most. It made the boat living, made it organic and coldly voracious, a stomach in mid-digestion. Even now he could hear it beneath him, that half-alive sound. No one else around him seemed to notice; sitting behind him, Umm Ibrahim sipped on a small vial of lemon juice to keep her nausea at bay and continued quietly reciting her foreign mantra.

Hello. I am pregnant. I will have baby on April twenty-eight. I need hospital and doctor to have safe baby. Please help.

"Please. Please," said a curly-haired Palestinian named Maher Ghandour, who, along with Walid Bin Walid, Kamal Roushdy and Mohamed, made up the nucleus of Amir's small corner of the boat. Of these passengers, Maher was the one who had first caught Amir's attention. He was thin and clean-shaven and dressed in a shirt that looked to be about a decade older than his twenty or so years. Bandages covered the tips of all his fingers.

"What?" Umm Ibrahim replied.

"Please, not *Blease. P-uh,* not *b-uh."*

"So you're an English teacher, are you?"

Maher raised his palm. "You're right—I'm sorry."

"Leave me alone," Umm Ibrahim said. "I have to learn it. They don't treat you well unless you speak their language."

Mohamed, the smugglers' apprentice, chuckled. "You want to speak their language? Take off that bedsheet you're wearing and throw it in the ocean. Their language isn't just about words."

"We're not coming from outer space," Umm Ibrahim said. "You're telling me they've never seen a Muslim before?"

"I'm telling you the exact opposite," Mohamed replied.

Amir could make no sense of the conversations taking place around him. Nor could he understand why so many people had lined up for this trip. Years earlier, Amir's father and Loud Uncle had taken him out on a small dhow. They sailed in the shadow of the massive military vessels near Tartus, keeping close to the shore and out of sight. There were only the three of them in the boat, the sun shining and the water calm. Amir had caught a fish that day, though now when he thought about it, he couldn't discount the possibility that, when his head was turned, Loud Uncle had hooked the little mackerel at the end of the line through sleight of hand. His father said he should get to know the sea because his people were of it, and although the drought had forced the Utus to abandon their orange groves and leave the coast for the cities inland, they'd always be seaside people.

But other than that one boat trip, the ferry across Aqaba and now this strange voyage, Amir had never spent time on the water. What he did remember of those two previous trips was that they had been nothing like this. On this boat the passengers pressed against one another, curled up into themselves. They sat with their faces down, pale in the light of their cell phone screens. They appeared in transit from themselves, concussed by the collision of the coming and the going, weightless as a tossed projectile at the apex of its arc.

Soon the rocking of the sea and the lateness of the

hour swayed most of the passengers to sleep. Amir sat amid darkness pierced by flashlight and silence pierced by snoring. Just above him, he caught sight of a sagging white sail hanging from one of the thick braided ropes that met at the mast. It hung limply, unmoved by the wind, and seemed to have no purpose at all; whatever propelled this ship, Amir knew, was the thing gurgling and rasping in the lower deck, the thing exhaling fumes. He could see it, almost, through a small crack in the boards beneath him, under slivers of flashlight that illuminated a tight-packed human armada of limbs and eyes, a pair of which caught sight of him and at which he could only stare back briefly before a great sense of indecency took hold and he forced himself to look away.

Chapter Nine

After

At the Hotel Xenios the poolside restaurant is crowded but free of its usual cacophony. The tourists sit under beach umbrellas, picking at their food and nursing elaborate tropical drinks. Vänna overhears little snippets of conversation about the wreck on the beach; the incident has ruined the tourists' day, confining them to the grounds of their hotel. She hears a middle-aged couple argue about whether to demand a refund.

After she pays for four cheeseburgers, she crosses the path back to the main road that leads to her home. At the intersection, she finds her sandals where she left them, the thin foam hot against her soles after an hour in the midday sun.

Not far from where the dirt path ends, Vänna sees two military trucks come up the road from the direction of her home. She recognizes the vehicles as those used by the loose assortment of military, police and coast guard officers charged with chasing down those who wash up on the island's shore alive. She stops and watches them pass.

The lead truck slows as it nears her; the passenger-side window rolls down. She recognizes immediately the broad, handsome face of the man who's been chosen to lead the island's efforts at rounding up the illegals, her mother's old friend Colonel Dimitri Kethros.

"What have you got there?" he asks, smiling and pointing to the plastic bag in her hand.

"Just lunch," Vänna replies. "Bought it from Xenios for Mom and Dad."

"Smells good. I don't suppose you bought any extra, by any chance?"

"No," Vänna says. "Just for the three of us."

Kethros eyes the bag in her hand and for a moment she thinks he can see into it somehow, that he can tell she's lying and from this lie will deduce exactly what she's up to. He has that look about him, of a man in possession of exactly as much information as he needs.

He is one of the largest men on the island—not fat and only a little taller than most, but well built, solid in a way she associates with military men even though many of the soldiers dispatched to the island are scrawny and barely out of their teens. In the thick straightness of his jawline and the width of his shoulders, the inverted triangle of him, he seems to have been built to excel at work that demands uniform and insignia. But he also has a charming smile, and this, more than any other facet of what he projects to the world, is what Vänna distrusts the most.

Kethros chuckles. "You can't blame a man for trying," he says. He pats the side of the passenger door and then waves her on. "Hurry up, before it gets cold."

She waits for the trucks to drive away. It is only then she notices that the second vehicle is not a jeep, but a kind of wagon, whose covered trunk looks like the sort of thing used to transport soldiers or prisoners. As soon as the vehicles are out of sight, Vänna sprints home.

She arrives to find her father sitting on one of the wicker chairs in the courtyard, and before she can go to the farmhouse, he calls her over. She can tell he's been drinking. He has no tolerance at all, and when drunk, assumes an outward posture entirely at odds with his inward disposition, or perhaps the two are inverted and he is finally, temporarily free to be what he really is. He leans back with his feet up on the table, a small, bitter grin on his face, and she knows at once her parents have been fighting again.

From childhood she has sensed it but only in recent years has she become fully cognizant of it—this weaponized emptiness between them, a void where once there might have existed tenderness, affection, a shared stake in shared happiness. Sometimes when she observes them following one of their fights, Vänna rejects outright that her parents are or ever have been in any kind of love. She thinks of them instead now as voyeurs, indecently intimate strangers.

Vänna walks to the courtyard. Her father taps the seat next to his. He tries to put the cap back on a bottle of Harborshine but stumbles and drops it onto the stone tiles. He smiles and shrugs.

"I brought some burgers from the Xenios," Vänna says. She sets one of the takeout boxes on the table and then picks up the bottle cap and a red plastic cup and an overturned ashtray off the floor.

"I know what you're thinking," her father says. "I'm not, though. Anyway, I wasn't. If she tells you I was, she's lying."

He is a small man, and in his smallness there is an ingrained element of youth that for years made him look a decade younger than he is. But now, in middle age, it has begun to bestow on him an air of ridiculousness, like the character in a movie Vänna once saw who aged four times faster than other children. His neatly parted hair is now slowly easing into a comb-over, but still looks strangely childlike.

Vänna sets one of the takeout containers on the table in front of him. He smiles and rubs her arm in gratitude but does not touch the food.

"I saw Colonel Kethros and some soldiers driving up the road when I was walking back," Vänna says, trying to sound uninterested. "You didn't see where they were coming from, did you?"

But her father doesn't seem to be listening at all. He stares out at the forest across the road.

"She can't tell cruel from strong," he says. "Never could."

Vänna doesn't reply. She's heard all this before, and knows what's coming next. She empties the ashtray in a nearby trash can and sets it back on the table. She waits.

"I'm so glad it was you who lived," her father says.

He pauses for a response from her that never comes. It's always the same story, the story he tells her because he can't bring himself to simply ask her to side with him against her mother.

"That's right," he continues. "There were two boys before you. They both died inside her."

She knows he won't stop until she plays along. Still, she says nothing.

"She only ever wanted boys," her father says. "She was so disappointed that the one who lived was you."

He watches her, smug with drunkenness, expectant.

"I'm not taking sides," she says.

"Who's asking you to take sides?" he replies. "I'm just telling you the truth. The truth doesn't take sides."

Vänna picks up the other takeout container. "I'm going to eat in the farmhouse," she says.

She crosses the courtyard. She sees mud prints in the grass, two-by-two in one direction, many in another, a tangled mess of strangers' tracks. There's a violence to it. She walks faster.

On her way to where she's left the boy in the outbuilding, she hears her parents' bedroom window swing open. She turns.

"Why were you gone so long?" her mother asks.

"The road was closed," Vänna replies. "There was a wreck on the beach and the soldiers blocked the path."

Her mother looks in the direction of the farmhouse. Vänna follows her eyes to find a half-open gym bag on the ground.

"He forgot to take it," Vänna's mother says.

"Who forgot?" Vänna asks.

Her father laughs. "Our brave protector," he says. "Who else?"

Vänna's mother ignores her husband. She stares at the bag a moment, thinking. Finally, she says, "Take it to Nimra, to that zoo she runs in the school gymnasium."

"What do I tell her?" Vänna asks.

"Don't tell her anything, just give it to her. Go, now."

Vänna walks to fetch the bag.

"Wait," her mother says. She disappears back into the bedroom and a moment later returns with a pair of yellow kitchen gloves. She throws them down to the yard, where they land at Vänna's feet.

In the farmhouse she finds the boy sitting up in the hayloft, a towel for a blanket, curled up, fetal. And seeing each other, both express a kind of relief that transcends the border of language between them, a lightening.

"I'm sorry," Vänna says, "They had soldiers everywhere. . . ."

She stops speaking. She walks to the open jug of maple syrup and closes the lid. She climbs the staircase and sits beside him. "Here," she says, sliding the takeout container in front of him. "Eat some real food."

The boy devours the meal. The caution with which he treated her during their first meeting momentarily disappears.

"Slow down—you'll be sick," she says. But he ignores her, and she is happy to watch him eat.

When he is done, she reaches over and gently wipes a smear of ketchup from the corner of his mouth with the tail of the towel he sits on.

"Good?" she asks, giving him a thumb's-up. He responds in kind.

She feels the afternoon sunlight against her back. She knows they have perhaps another two or three hours before dusk, and her thoughts turn to more pressing things. In the back of the farmhouse there lie in boarded stacks the makings of a twin bed. She considers rummaging around for her grandparents' old toolbox and putting the bed together herself, but quickly she decides against it.

"Come," she says. "I'm going to take you to meet someone."

She stands and picks up the bag her mother told her to deliver, then motions for the boy to follow. She opens the front door and glances outside at the courtyard, where her father sits in his chair with his eyes closed. She turns to the boy and puts her finger against her lips in a motion requesting silence; he nods.

Light as thieves, they move around the courtyard and to the back of the house. As they cross the backyard, Dadge the sheepdog lifts her head in faint recognition, but quickly loses interest. They climb over a dilapidated wooden fence and pass into the remains of the old harborberry grove, muddled now with weeds and otherwise barren. With Vänna leading, the two children walk in the direction of a long, tin-roofed building on the other side of the grove—once a high school gymnasium and now a temporary pen for those without country.

Chapter Ten

Before

I t was Teddy's shift again. Amir watched him struggle in the wheelhouse. He was a short, skinny man, his slightness of frame exaggerated by the ship's oversize wheel, which seemed to turn of its own volition exactly in the opposite direction of wherever Teddy wished to steer. The boat tilted and bobbed and every few times the starboard side dropped down from the apex of a wave, a spray of mist came through the broken window. Still, Teddy held fast, and in the darkness, without any point of reference on which to fix, it was just as likely as not the boat was going where he intended it to go.

Maher looked up from his book. "You want some help?" he asked.

Teddy shrugged. "There's not much to help with." He tapped the cloudy glass-bubbled compass attached to the helm's dash, inside of which a needle sputtered wildly. "Just keep it on *N*, right?"

"I guess so," Maher said.

It took only a few sentences for the passengers overhearing the conversation to become aware that of those near the stern of the boat, the Eritrean and the Palestinian were the most fluent speakers of English, and quietly many made note of this fact, in case it proved useful upon landfall.

Teddy noticed Amir watching him. He smiled. "Maybe you can help," he said, waving the boy over.

Amir looked up at Umm Ibrahim, uncertain. "Go ahead, baby," she said. "It's fine."

He stood up and walked around the mass of bodies to the wheelhouse. It was only a half-covered thing, the roof planks gnawed and cracked, green with streaks of mildew. The compartment, no bigger than a broom closet, smelled of licorice and salt water. It was a too-tight space for even one person, but in this upturning of the world, it felt comforting to be so confined; it was the sight of the endless open sea that brought on claustrophobia.

"Hold tight," Teddy said, wrapping Amir's fingers around a handle. "Don't let it move you; you're the boss."

Instantly it moved him, the counterclockwise rotation so sudden he was nearly lifted off his feet trying to keep hold. Teddy laughed and righted course. "We'll do it together," he said.

Walid, sitting nearby, rapped the side of the wheelhouse. "No play, no play," he said in English. "Make serious."

Teddy chuckled. He pointed to the nighttime darkness that surrounded them. "Are you worried we'll get lost?"

Mohamed gestured at Walid to quiet down. "It's fine," he said. "Just mind your own business."

"This isn't a time for joking around," Walid protested. "We're not out here to play."

"It doesn't matter," Mohamed said. "When you get to the other side, then you can pretend to be a walking funeral—that's what they'll be waiting for. But right now, it doesn't matter if you play or dance or whatever." He pointed to an old man sitting portside, quietly reciting fifteen attributes of God from the end of a Quranic chapter. "Just be like this guy. Just mind your own business."

"His steering is my business," Walid said.

Mohamed shook his head. "Fuck it," he said. "I've had enough of this." He reached into his pocket and for an instant a look of complete terror crossed Walid's face, until Mohamed pulled out a rusted skeleton key. He motioned to Teddy.

"Hey, take this," he said in English, tossing the key his way. "You make open small door inside. You give."

Teddy opened the small cupboard below the dash. Inside he found a small mug with a Nefertiti-bust handle and an unlabeled bottle three-quarters full of something white and cloudy. He passed these things down, and from passenger to passenger they found their way to Mohamed, who poured a mugful and gave it to Walid.

"You people like arak, right?"

"Can't stand the stuff," Walid said, declining. "It tastes like candy gone rotten."

"Who gives a shit what it tastes like?" Mohamed replied. "C'mon, I need there to be at least one more real man on this boat."

Walid took the cup. He sipped the liquor, he winced.

"There you go," said Mohamed, who'd learned over the years exactly how to ply a man such as Walid into compliance. He spoke to the others nearby, and made sure Walid heard it. "Now this is someone I can drink with, someone with a pair of balls."

Kamal leaned over. "I'll take a sip," he said.

"Fuck off," Mohamed replied.

The boat meandered through the empty sea. In time Amir grew tired and let go of the wheel. He sat on an upturned bucket by the foot of the wheelhouse and listened to Teddy and Maher speak in a language he couldn't understand, as all the while Walid grew more and more tipsy, Mohamed occasionally refilling his cup.

"How long ago did you leave Eritrea?" Maher asked.

"Eight months," Teddy replied.

"And only now you're getting on the boat?"

"There was a lot before the boat. There was leaving the country, then finding someone who would take me, then crossing the desert, then getting into Egypt, then finding someone else who would take me, then this."

"So why did you leave?" Maher asked. "Military?"

Teddy nodded. At the sound of the word *military,* Mohamed sat up.

"He's with the army?" he asked Maher.

"They've got mandatory conscription," Maher replied. "Everybody's with the army."

"Not soldier," Teddy said in broken Arabic. "Mathematician."

"You're at war over there, in your country?" Mohamed asked.

Teddy shrugged. "Depends what you mean by war."

Amir listened, and at the sound of the word was drawn into a memory of home.

His father once said war was something that happened to people but also alongside them. From where he sat in the Utus' living room back in Homs, reclined on a honey-colored Louis XV chair, that particular aesthetic of decor which to an older generation of Arabs symbolized not only an aspirational Westernness but also a time before the worst of things, Amir's father pointed out the window to the shattered end of the street. The week prior, not long after military planes had littered propaganda from the sky, little square papers that fell to the ground like dying birds, the barrel bombs had torn open one of the buildings nearby.

In the evening the shells explode and overnight it rains and in the morning the children swim in the craters, Amir's father said. People live—what else is there to do?

They were three brothers who, in Amir's view of the world, together comprised the entirety of manhood. His whole life, he had associated Loud Uncle with brashness and Quiet Uncle with timidity but ever since he heard him say it, he associated his father with that statement— *What else is there to do?*

He was forgettable in the way many good men were, not physically imposing but of dignified bearing, a posture he adjusted according to the import of his company. In the last years of his life, before he was taken, he wore a short, neatly trimmed beard, black but littered with minute red hairs his friends and neighbors complimented as being a trait of the Prophet, a beard that when he wore his skullcap to Friday prayers made him appear a pious man, and when he didn't, made him appear cosmopolitan. He made do with an uncooperative left arm, a remnant of childhood calamity from a time before the drought, when the Utus still farmed a vast orange grove near the sea: while picking rocks, he'd stumbled and shattered his humerus on a half-buried shovel blade. He screamed, feverish, for days and his mother and siblings pleaded, but Amir's grandfather refused to take him into town because the only doctor there was a Frenchman, and he'd rather his son die than be fixed by a Frenchman. And so he'd learned to live with it, as he'd learned to live with drought and displacement and now a war that raged alongside him. What else was there to do?

Perhaps this is what made him stand out, the day after another half-dozen children were arrested for spray-painting slogans on the walls and swept into the underground prisons, and Loud Uncle convinced him to march with him in the protest, and when the screaming and shooting subsided they were never to be seen again. Perhaps it was not the presence of a revolutionary at a revolution that so enraged the secret police who took them, but the presence of an ordinary man.

"What kind of mathematics did you study?" Maher asked.

"Big numbers," Teddy replied.

"Big numbers?"

"You ever hear of tree functions? Graham's number?"

Maher shook his head. "Sorry."

"It's okay—nobody has," Teddy replied. "Let's see. You know how to add, yes?"

"Sure."

"And multiplication is just adding again and again, right?"

"Sure."

"And when you take something to the power of something, that's just multiplying again and again, right?"

"Sure."

"That's one way you can get to big numbers," Teddy said. "Just keep going one more level up."

"A million billion," Walid said, sleepy-eyed and smiling. "A billion million billion." The two men ignored him.

"So what do you do with these numbers?" Maher asked.

"Sometimes you use them for proofs, or you try to find the next big number, like with primes, just to show you can. Sometimes you do nothing with them," Teddy replied. "It's about imagination. When you have a number that's bigger than all the atoms in the universe put together, what does that mean? How do you think about something that's too big to think about?"

"A gabrillion," Walid said to himself, giggling.

Maher held his book up to Teddy, almost apologetically. "I never really understood numbers," he said.

"But words?"

"Yes, words."

"And you prefer them to people?" Teddy asked.

"Very much."

"Then you understand."

Walid stumbled up, making a motion with his hand in imitation of a jabbering mouth. "Blah blah blah," he said. "Enough of this talking. We need music.

"You," he said, pointing at Kamal. "You young people have music on your phones, right?"

"Sit down, man, you're drunk," Kamal replied.

"You do, you all do, I know it." Walid leaned in Kamal's direction, holding a stranger's shoulder for support. "Play something."

"I have one song on this phone," Kamal said. "It's by Amr Diab and I downloaded it for my uncle and it sucks."

"Amr Diab? I thought that guy was dead," Mohamed said.

"Amr Diab will never die," Kamal said. "He goes to a clinic in Brazil every year where they change out all his organs."

"Play the goddamn song!" Walid yelled.

"Fine, fine." Kamal turned up the volume on his phone and set it down halfway between where he and Walid sat. Through mediocre speakers the sound of the classical guitars came out as static and the accordion as an old modem and hardly anyone could make out the voice behind it all, the whole while yodeling, *Habibi, habibi.*

Walid clapped his hands in approval, and by the time the song ended he was belly-dancing in place, oblivious to the growing amusement of his neighbors, and by the time he had Kamal play it a fourth time in a row, even the people who had never heard it before and didn't speak Arabic could sing the chorus, and Walid was up now and dancing with his tie like a bandanna around his head, and Mohamed smiled and shook his head and Amir, caught up in the silliness of it all, laughed and sang along.

Chapter Eleven

After

Vänna and Amir cross the harborberry grove. Most of the grove is barren but a few plants survive; here and there the pits of the fleshy green and black fruit litter the ground. It grows nowhere else but the island and during harvest season sets loose in the air a smell like the inside of a pickling jar.

They walk in the direction of the repurposed gymnasium. The building, which once belonged to a nearby high school but has been cordoned off to form a temporary holding center, has about it an air of passive siege. Both the gymnasium and the soccer field adjacent to it are lined with a fence originally designed to hold insolent teenagers, and even though its height has been doubled since the facility's repurposing, it still looks feeble. Police officers and coast guard troops patrol the perimeter, as alien to the people inside the facility as those people are to them.

From where the grove ends at the bank of a small ditch, Vänna can see rows of small camping tents that cover the soccer field. Young men duck in and out of the tents, and a few sleep outside on the browning grass, taking in the sunlight after the previous night's freeze.

She sees a young soldier standing at the front gate. She can tell right away he's a mainlander. It occurs to her then that she has no idea how many of the men who chased the boy to her house know what he looks like. She stops at the edge of the ditch and turns to the child. She points to the guard at the gate and then makes a motion of covering her mouth with her hand. The boy nods.

They cross the ditch and walk up to the gate. The guard shakes from his stupor and observes them with a kind of disdainful curiosity.

"You can't come in here," he says. "Go around the far road to get to the school."

"We're not going to the school," Vänna replies.

It has been more than a year since these young uniformed men arrived on her side of the island. Like all soldiers, they were trained for warfare but, once dispatched here, what they found was not what most of them thought of as war. To become soldiers required they be rid of a certain kind of human reticence. The pulling of a trigger was in the end a rote, mechanical movement—anyone could be taught it. The difficult thing, the necessary thing, was to first kill off the instinct not to pull it. A person freed of this instinct requires the full theater of war, its protective mythology, without which this particular absence of restraint descends into sociopathy. But no such theater exists in these camps. For years these soldiers have been taught to wield hammers, only to come to the island and find not nails, but glass.

"My brother and I live across the road," Vänna says, pointing past the unused grove. "My mother is friends with Madame El Ward—she sent us to give her this bag."

She volunteers no further information. The guard looks from the ruined bag to the grove.

"Leave it here," he says.

Vänna shakes her head. "This bag belonged to an illegal Colonel Kethros arrested near our house. He asked my mother to make sure it was delivered to this facility."

She waits to see whether the soldier buys it. But he doesn't, she can already tell, and too quickly into the silence that follows, she blurts out, "You can call him if you want."

The soldier opens a small metal phone box bolted to the side of the guard kiosk. He punches a number.

"Don't move," he says to Vänna as he waits for an answer.

Vänna prepares to run. She eases slightly to be closer to the boy, who seems to have no idea what's happening. She chooses a direction—south, toward the cloudstone caves, that vast underground network in which at least one tourist gets lost every week, down into the stalactite caverns slick with condensation, across the underground rivers, to places where they'll never be found. It's only a couple of miles away; they can make it.

She knows it's all nonsense. They won't get twenty feet.

"Hello? Alec? Where's Kethros?" The soldier shouts into the receiver. His face twists into annoyed confusion as he tries to make out the answer across bad static.

"It's your job to know," he says. "Listen, forward me to

his deputy's cell. . . . It's on the paper taped to the phone you're holding. . . . I don't know if it's pound or star, just pick one, for fuck's sake."

Even the children can hear the sound of static disappearing as the line goes dead. The soldier slams the receiver back, picks it up and begins to dial again, then stops. He reaches into the kiosk and picks up two visitors' lanyards. He hands them to Vänna.

"Go inside the big building only, you understand? Don't go out into the field, and don't talk to any of them."

Vänna nods. She takes Amir by the hand; they pass through the gate.

They cross a dirt yard, trampled by generations of children's feet, and enter the gymnasium, whose exterior has been stripped of all signage related to the adjacent high school. Nothing indicates what the facility is now being used for, and so the wide, squat building stands absent public identity, a nowhere place.

They walk inside. Vänna leads the way upstairs to Madame El Ward's office. It's a room of three walls, pressed against a narrow steel walkway, which overlooks the basketball and volleyball courts below. In place of a fourth wall, the room, which once served as a storage space for sports equipment, opens directly onto the walkway, offering a view of the whole gymnasium.

They find Madame Nimra El Ward at her cluttered desk, arguing with someone on the phone. Vänna knocks on the side of the wall; Madame El Ward turns and, not seeing the boy accompanying Vänna, waves her in.

The children enter and sit on an old couch on the other

side of the room. Madame El Ward's attention turns back to her phone conversation.

"We're going in circles," she says. "I'm not saying you didn't deliver it, I'm saying you may as well have not."

Vänna and Amir listen, though one doesn't understand the language being spoken and the other doesn't understand the context. They sit quietly, taking in the room. On the floor and the table there are boxes of identical files, some bulging with testimonials and photographs and notarized government documents, others completely empty. Each folder is labeled with a long identification number.

"The issue is that it came in the same truck, Mr. Perdiou," Madame El Ward says. "It came in the same truck that delivered the generator fuel yesterday, and which your employees didn't bother cleaning between deliveries. You could see the light reflecting on the surface of the water when we poured it out."

Amir grows fidgety. He stands and walks over to the edge of the steel walkway. He looks out at the gymnasium below. The floor is marked with the straight and curving lines, the boundaries of myriad courts, but the nets and goals and almost all other sports equipment have been removed to make way for rows and rows of low steel cots. Only the basketball nets, which descend from the ceiling, remain.

Amir watches a girl standing under one of the nets. She looks a little younger than Amir, or perhaps the same age but a little stunted. She stands directly under the net, a small red ball in her hands. There's a paper bracelet wrapped around the girl's right wrist. Amir watches as she silently tosses the ball upward through the bottom of the net, scoring in reverse. The ball floats upward in a perfectly vertical arc, as though on a string, and then falls back down through the net and into her hands. Over and over again. Each time, the ball doesn't deviate an inch from its perfect arc, the net completely unmoved.

"You understand *perfectly* what the problem is," Madame El Ward yells into the receiver. "The question of why you need to pretend otherwise is one you should take up with your conscience, Mr. Perdiou. In the meantime, you owe me a day's worth of uncontaminated drinking water. Good-bye."

Madame El Ward hangs up the phone. She puts her head down and exhales deeply, kneading her shoulders, trying to squeeze the knots out.

"I'm sorry, Vänna," she says, turning. "Some of these people, you have to hold their hand and show them how to be human."

She stops. For the first time, she looks at Amir.

"The accident at Revel Beach this morning," Vänna says. "I think he came on that boat."

Madame El Ward doesn't reply. She has seen so many over the last year: alone, malnourished; orphaned by war or by sea; made into the undercurrents of themselves, broken in ways that rendered them unable to continue as children and yet a part of them left childlike forever. She has seen so many and every time the sight freezes her in terrible reverence.

"They said no one survived."

She approaches the boy, kneels down, places her hand on the side of his face. He flinches.

"Hello," she says. "What's your name?" Her ability to speak his language, and with something resembling his accent, takes Amir aback. But quickly he regains his composure.

"David," he says.

"Are you sure that's your name?" she asks. "You can tell me the truth. I'm not here to hurt you."

"Of course I'm sure," Amir replies. "You think I don't know my own name?"

Madame El Ward smiles. "Of course, of course," she says. "I'm very sorry, David. My name is Nimra. Where are you from, David?"

The boy says nothing.

"Did you come here on a boat?"

Amir hesitates. Madame El Ward runs her hand through his hair; she feels the salt.

"There's no need to be afraid," she says. She leans in close to the boy, imparting a whispered secret. "We're on an island, David. Everyone comes here on a boat." She smiles.

She goes over and opens one of her desk drawers. She retrieves a chocolate bar and hands it to him.

"Tell me," she says. "Did you come here alone?"

Amir shakes his head. "I came with my uncle. I was on the top part of the boat and he was in the bottom part."

Madame El Ward stops smiling. "That's good," she says. "That's . . ."

Something about the way her expression changes, the

way the cots line the floor downstairs, the way the girl tosses the ball over and over and over again—Amir turns and runs.

Quickly Vänna grabs him and, a second later, Madame El Ward has her arms around him too.

"I don't like it here," he screams. "Don't make me stay here."

"It's going to be all right," Madame El Ward says. "I promise, you don't have to stay here. Just take a deep breath. It's okay to be scared. I know this is all new, but I'm here to help you."

She reaches behind her to the bottom of a nearby shelving unit, on which sit stacks of cardboard boxes. Unlike most of the room's contents, these boxes are filled not with folders but with all manner of discarded relics from previous journeys—folded family photographs, half-used coloring books, sparkly pencil cases, hair bands. One box contains nothing but broken cell phones. She rummages through the boxes, searching.

"How did you find him?" she asks Vänna.

"He came running out of the forest this morning," Vänna replies. "Up from the beach. There were men chasing him, coast guard officers and police."

"Just him?"

"Yes."

Madame El Ward pauses. She looks out past where Amir stands, at the wide hollow of the gymnasium and at the cots that line the floor; the places where days have been etched in the walls with penknives and fingernails, the places where bedsheets were hung from the beams.

She was Vänna's French teacher once, before she

took early retirement. They are neighbors too, in a relative sense, their houses both near the easternmost shore, about three miles apart. Like Vänna, she was born here, the only daughter of immigrants who made the same journey in a less hostile time. Vänna's mother once said you could see it plainly on her face, the real origins of her, in her eyes and her hair, but also in the way she was, in the marrow of her. And hearing Madame El Ward described this way, Vänna could not help but think of ancestry as a kind of shackle one could never fully unclasp, an umbilical cord that, no matter how deeply cut, could never be severed.

Early on, when the boats began to arrive more frequently, Madame El Ward set her retirement on hold in order to volunteer with aid and translation at the island's hastily built migrant camp. And in time, as the government offloaded more and more responsibility to whichever aid group was willing to take it on, she came to oversee the whole facility, the place where those who survived the passage were taken to wait while, slowly and with well-honed inefficiency, the system considered their appeals for asylum.

"Can you take him?" Vänna asks.

"We can," Madame El Ward replies. "By law he has to come here. The ministry would fire me if I . . ." She pauses. "Tell me, those men who chased him, did any of them see him with you? Do they know you took him here?"

"No," Vänna says. "I hid him in our farmhouse. I told the guard outside he was my brother."

"Your parents didn't see him?"

"No."

Madame El Ward stands. She walks to the window and looks outside. A soldier patrols the perimeter fence, a pair of headphones in his ears. She closes the blinds.

"Vänna, do you know what happens to people here?" she asks. "I mean, do you know how this process works?"

Vänna shrugs. "They come here, they apply for—I don't know—passports? Then they get them and they go somewhere on the mainland."

Madame El Ward nods. "Something like that. But it doesn't always happen that way. Sometimes they're made to live in places like this gymnasium for a very long time, sometimes they're sent to places . . . Listen, I want you to do something for me, Vänna. I want you take this boy somewhere."

Madame El Ward opens a desk drawer and pulls out a small paper map of the island. She shows it to Vänna.

"Do you know the place at the very northeastern tip of the island?" she asks. "Have you ever gone there?"

"Where the broken lighthouse is?" Vänna replies.

"Yes, where the broken lighthouse is. I want you to go there. Right after the main road narrows for the second time, you'll see a small path on the left side of the road. It leads through the terrace trees and down to an abandoned dock. I want you to take him there. Can you do that?"

"What do we do when we get there?"

"There's a man I know who runs a boat to the mainland," Madame El Ward says. "Once a week, Sunday at noon. It's not something he's allowed to do, and he'll get in a lot of trouble if he's found out, so you need to keep this just between you and me. But if you can get this boy there before the ferryman leaves on Sunday, he can take him where there's a community of people from the same place he came from, a community of people who can help him. He stands a better chance that way, Vänna. Do you understand?"

Vänna nods.

Madame El Ward kneels back down to Amir. "Tell me," she says, pointing at Vänna. "Has this one been treating you all right?"

"Yes," he says shyly.

"You sure?"

"Yes."

"Good. Now, if it's okay with you, I want you two to go on a little trip together. I think you'll have a lot of fun and I think afterward you'll be able to get off this island. Would you like that?"

"My uncle said we'd go back together after the boat trip," Amir says.

"I think he's on his way there too. Soon we'll see about getting you two reunited, but for now it's important to get you away from those men who were chasing you this morning. And you don't want to stay here, right?"

Amir shakes his head.

She picks a small child's backpack from one of the boxes on the shelf and begins to fill it with books. Then she passes it to Vänna.

"It's the translation picture book we give the children here," she says. "And a couple of comic books, fairy tales, that sort of thing. It'll keep him occupied."

Vänna takes the bag. "Sunday at noon," she says.

"That's right," Madame El Ward replies. "Just keep him safe and out of sight for two days. I don't just mean out of the sight of the coast guard and the police, I mean everyone."

They hear a sound outside: trucks at the gate. Madame El Ward peeks out from behind the blinds. She sees two military vehicles at the driveway. The guard swings the gate open; they drive inside.

"Go, quickly," Madame El Ward says. "Look for Markos downstairs, and ask him to let you out through the back gate. Stay off the main roads, and stay safe."

"All right."

"Just two days, that's all," Madame El Ward says. "If you can keep him hidden for two days and get him on that ferry, if you can keep them from putting him in the system or sending him back, he'll have a chance."

Madame El Ward waves good-bye. Amir waves back. The children leave just a few moments before Madame El Ward hears the front door open and the syncopated sound of boots climbing the steel staircase. A moment later, Colonel Kethros enters her office.

Chapter Twelve

Before

Amist of salt water sprayed the stern; Amir's legs itched. He pulled his shirt over his knees, stretching it until it resembled a nightgown. For hours after he returned to his place near Umm Ibrahim, he'd struggled to get comfortable. Each passing wave knocked his head back against the boards or to the sides, where it collided with Umm Ibrahim's knees. It wasn't long before the boat's ceaseless movement acquainted all the passengers with their immediate neighbors, and erased some of the distinction between where one body ended and another began.

So too had Amir become acclimated, unconsciously, to the smell of diesel fumes that now permeated the deck, and the growling of the engine deep in the gut of the old fishing boat. Subjected to these things for hours, the senses rendered them no more noticeable than the color of air.

Umm Ibrahim removed from her small purse a sandwich bag containing a few browning apple slices. She ate one and offered one to Amir. He shook his head.

"You'll get sick if you don't eat," Umm Ibrahim said. The heat had caused many others on the boat to take off some of their clothes, but she had not removed her niqab. Still, she had become familiar to Amir in other ways, by the color of her eyes and the sound of her voice and the bruising knock of her knee against his temple.

"My mother says I shouldn't eat fruit unless I wash it," Amir replied. "Otherwise I'll get germs."

Walid, trying to rub the hangover out of his temples, sighed. "Lady, what are you doing giving food away?" he said, pointing at Umm Ibrahim's belly. "You already have a child to look after."

"What do you care what I do with my own food?" Umm Ibrahim replied. She retrieved a small bottle of water from her purse and handed it, along with an apple slice, to Amir. "Here," she said. "Use a little of this to wash it off, then it won't have any germs, right?"

Amir took the bottle. He stood and leaned over the gunwale and rinsed the apple slice. With his back turned, he did not see the look of overwhelming rage that momentarily came over Walid's face.

"Remember this," Walid said to Umm Ibrahim, "when you run out, when you're stuck drinking the sea."

Umm Ibrahim came to respond but was interrupted by an electronic chime, repeating in rapid succession.

Kamal reached into his pocket. "Sorry, sorry," he said to his neighbors. He looked at the screen.

"Looks like we have a signal," he said.

Suddenly the stern broke out in wild activity. The passengers quickly turned their phones on and tried to catch the electronic current in the air. For a brief moment, the sound of the wheezing engine was drowned out by an atonal orchestra of beeps and jingles. It moved up the boat like a wave, until even the passengers at the very edge of the bow had their phones out.

"Be careful, be careful!" Mohamed yelled. "Stay in your places. There's no signal out here, it's just a mistake."

Quickly it became clear that whatever possessed Kamal's phone was a fleeting thing, now gone. Slowly the passengers lowered their hands and turned off their phones and returned to their places, dejected.

"You raised everyone's hopes for nothing," Walid said, leaning over Kamal's shoulder to look at his phone screen. "What did you receive, then?"

"It's from the phone company," Kamal said. "It says I've run out of credits."

Kamal turned the phone off. He sat back next to Maher, who'd never taken his eyes off his book. He watched him, watched the yellow-stained bandages that covered his fingers.

"What did you use?" Kamal asked.

"Acid," Maher replied.

"Did it hurt?"

"Yes."

"Why did they turn you away, the first time?"

"Does it matter?"

Kamal shrugged. "Just making conversation, brother."

Maher returned to his book. He set it low on his lap now, the spine braced against his crossed ankles, his bandaged fingers hidden behind the pages.

"What did you do, back in Gaza?" Kamal asked.

Maher closed his book. "I was a student. English literature," he replied.

"English literature?"

"That's right. What about you?"

Kamal shrugged. "One year of an economics degree, then professional revolutionary, then guest of the government."

Mohamed put down his cell phone, on which he'd been playing a game of Snake. "Which prison?" he asked.

"Scorpion," Kamal replied. "Thirteen months."

"That's a good one." Mohamed pointed northward. "The Westerners have heard of that one. While you were in there, did they—you know—make less of a man out of you?"

"What the hell is wrong with you?" Kamal said.

Mohamed shook his head. "Brother, I don't give a shit, I'm just saying—when you get over there, tell them they did. Tell them they used the stick, the electrodes. Be graphic."

"Make them feel uncomfortable, that's what you mean?"

"No, none of that stuff makes them feel uncomfortable," Mohamed said. "It makes them feel enlightened."

Dusk descended. Hoping to ease the kink in his neck, Amir stood and wedged himself between Umm Ibrahim and her neighbor, who both sat on the wooden benches just below the gunwale. Squeezed between them, he looked out at the white-green flesh of the sea. There was a scent to it, the salt that in the nostrils registered as a kind of burning. Gently the *Calypso* rose and fell with the sweep of the waves, each departing with a wet slap against the hull. Amir cast about the horizon, in search of land or life. He saw none.

It entranced him, the echo-breathing emptiness of the sea. Here or there a gull cried out, and if he leaned upward and let his eyes go limp he was able to shape the contours of the clouds into all manner of strange creatures, but these were only fleeting breaks in the nothingness.

He saw something moving, an off-black bruise on the water. It swam alongside the boat at perfectly symmetrical speed, never breaking the surface. For a second he thought it might be a shark. The previous evening, someone on his side of the boat had said this region was infested with them, and that they chased the boats because now that they'd gotten a taste, they'd turned insatiable.

Then he realized it was just the muted shadow of the limp white sail hanging off the mast behind him.

"Did you ever try the official way?" Kamal asked Maher. "I heard they have a special system for Palestinians."

Maher chuckled. "They sure do," he said. "How about you?"

Kamal took a small green card out of his wallet and handed it to Maher.

Maher inspected the card, back and front, astounded. "They gave you one? And you decided to come on this boat?"

"Of course they didn't give me one," Kamal replied. "It's a forgery. There's a guy in Sayyidah Zaynab who'll make you one in fifteen minutes for a hundred pounds."

"Huh," Maher said.

"I waited on the real thing three years," Kamal said. "I gave them all the papers they wanted, I told them the name of the officer who did it, I showed them the marks on my back, I went to see the man in that office—what do they call it, the boss of refugees?"

"High commissioner . . ."

"Every day. Every day. And then one day they said I'd left one of the fields empty on a form. I said, 'What field?' They said, 'Apartment number.' I said, 'I live in a house.' They said, 'It doesn't matter—the new policy is if there's any blank field at all, it's an automatic rejection.' And that was that."

"How come they took your application in the first place?" Maher asked. "I thought you couldn't apply in the country you're from."

"My parents are Iraqi," said Kamal.

"You don't sound Iraqi," Maher replied.

"Brother, I couldn't point out Iraq on a map."

"Did you have a babysitter?" Maher asked.

"A British guy," Kamal replied. "A man named David."

"I had a David too," Walid said. "British guy. He used to bring gifts every time he came to visit, those tote bags you see everywhere. Nice guy. Perfectly useless, but nice."

Maher pointed at Kamal's forged identity card. "You should probably throw that out," he said. "The worst thing you can do when we land is let them see your name on that thing."

"What difference does it make?" Kamal asked. "When we get there, it won't matter if it's real or fake."

"I don't mean that," Maher said. "I mean because it has your name. You've got to give them a name that sounds like one of theirs. They hear 'Mohamed,' 'Ahmed,' anything like that, and it's a different world altogether."

"He's right," Mohamed said. "Every time we do this, all you idiots bring blankets, medicine, cell phones. One man—a grown man—tried to bring his puppy. But nobody ever thinks to bring a big shiny cross. They see you coming off the boat with one of those things hanging around your neck, it'll do you more good than all the ID cards in the world."

He pointed at the passengers huddled around him. "If you have any sense at all, you'll never give the Westerners your real names. Pick something common—George, Jack, Peter, Michael, Nicholas. Pick a saint, any saint."

Umm Ibrahim nodded. "I chose Sylvia."

Mohamed chuckled. "Good luck with that," he said.

The evening darkened, the boat drifted. Walid stood and lit the flashlight lantern. For a while the stern was quiet, until Amir spoke.

"Where are we going?" he asked.

The passengers around him looked at one another, but none offered an answer.

"The old man said this was a short trip, and we'd be back soon," Amir said. "But we've been out here forever. Where are we going?"

Kamal turned to Mohamed. "What's this boy doing on the boat?" he asked. "How did he get on here all alone?"

"He's not all alone," Mohamed replied. "He's got some

uncle or something down below. He couldn't afford to put himself and the kid up here, but that's his problem."

Mohamed turned to Amir. "Listen, in a while we'll be off this boat and then you and your uncle will find plenty of people to help you do whatever it is you want to do—stay, leave, open a nightclub, I don't care. Until then, just keep quiet and don't ask any more questions."

Kamal stood and began to approach the smugglers' apprentice, before Maher restrained him.

"What's wrong with you?" Kamal yelled. "This whole time he has family on the boat, and you won't let them sit together? Why, because of a few dollars? Don't you have a conscience?"

Mohamed let out a high whistle. "A conscience, everybody!" he said, waving at the passengers surrounding him as though egging them on to join the conversation. "Our much-esteemed revolutionary wants to talk to us about a conscience."

Kamal shoved Maher's hand aside. He took two steps before Mohamed eased his jacket open to reveal a small pistol holstered at his side. At the sight of the weapon, Kamal stopped; the other passengers quieted.

"Conscience, brother, is the enemy of survival," Mohamed said. "Sit down."

Neither Kamal nor any of the passengers near him responded, and for a few minutes there was only the wheezing of the engine and the wrinkled sigh of the wind through the sagging sail. Maher returned to his book, Walid and Kamal sat back down and stared out at the endless sea and Umm Ibrahim retrieved her folded paper and began once more to recite the English plea she struggled to memorize:

Hello. I am pregnant. I will have baby on April twenty-eight. I need hospital and doctor to have safe baby. Please help.

Night fell.

Chapter Thirteen

After

For a few seconds the colonel simply stands there, ignoring Madame El Ward entirely, observing the pictures decorating her office wall.

They are unframed, creased with folding marks, and haphazardly attached to the wall with tape or pushpins. They are pictures of men and women and children posing by the landmarks of their adopted homes—here a young woman playing with perspective, holding up a tower; there a bundled-up child, making wings in a snowdrift. Pictures of the ones who made it.

"Hello, Colonel," Madame El Ward says. "Didn't expect to see you today."

Kethros smiles. He sits on the couch. There's an ease of place about him, a presumed sense of ownership over his surroundings.

"You know, I never get any complaints from this place," he says. "Everywhere else I station my men, they complain—the civilian administrators aren't following the rules, the civilian administrators aren't following the rules, like a broken record. But never here. You should be proud; the first thing to go in times like these is good form."

"What can I do for you, Colonel?" Madame El Ward asks.

"Two things," Kethros replies. "First, I was hoping you'd indulge me while I tell you the story of my day."

He leans back on the couch and puts his hands on the back of his head. "By now you've heard about the mess at Revel Beach."

"I have," Madame El Ward replies. "One of your boys called me and said—what were his words again?—Don't bother freeing up any beds."

"Which is tactless, I suppose, but true," Kethros says. "Or so we thought this morning. Turns out we were wrong. A child survived. My soldiers gave chase but lost the scent somewhere around Marianne Hermes's house."

The colonel sits up, motioning with his hands as though he were getting to the most important part of the story.

"Later on, a couple showed up a few miles south along the coast in a flimsy little raft. When we caught them, they claimed they were from Syria, which is pretty well a made-up place now, so many of them lie about being from there. Anyway, they also passed through Marianne's place. She called us to come get them."

"I don't see what any of this has to do with me, Colonel," Madame El Ward says.

"Yes you do," Kethros replies. "After we picked them up, we returned to the field office near the Hotel Xenios. And when we got there, one of my soldiers told me that Marianne's daughter had come around earlier, asking if we found anybody in the wreckage of that fishing boat, anybody by the name Utu. Why would she do that?"

"I'm not a mind reader, Colonel."

"Where did they go, Nimra?"

"I don't know what you're talking about."

Kethros exhales deeply. He stands and walks to the window, his false leg evident in the asymmetry of his gait. He opens the blinds.

"Let's not play this game," he says. "Marianne told me the daughter was coming here, and that idiot I've got stationed outside just let a couple of kids through."

"I have more important things to do, Colonel, than help you with this hunch you seem to have," Madame El Ward replies. "I've got six hundred people in a camp made for three hundred, and all of them are owed a day's drinking water. Maybe you want to help with that instead?"

"Did you fill out the requisition forms properly?"

Madame El Ward grabs a sheet of paper off her desk and holds it up. "Of course I filled it out properly. Every day 'properly' changes, and every day I still fill it out properly. What possible good does it do to make them suffer like this? What purpose does it serve? Even ordinary criminals don't get treated this way."

"Ordinary criminals commit ordinary crimes," the colonel replies.

Madame El Ward points to the gymnasium below. "We have children who can't sleep through the night, we have people who don't talk anymore, who try to slit their wrists with canned-food lids. This place is hell."

"Hell? Really?" Kethros walks to the edge of the railing and surveys the courts below.

"You know, back when I was a peacekeeper, we had a problem," he says. "If I'm being honest, it was our fault. You see, when they tell you to keep the peace in a killing field, what they really mean is, Do nothing. And when you have soldiers with nothing to do, they tend to develop bad habits. So we had this problem with bribes.

"I tried to put a stop to it, but my superiors told me, You have to let that sort of thing go, because you have no choice; there's nothing quite as useless as a perfectionist in wartime. I think they were wrong; I think wartime is the only place for a perfectionist. But the problem is, at first people would pay a few dollars here and there just to get through a checkpoint with less hassle, and so it would get around that the going rate at that particular checkpoint was a few dollars. But then you have people who've got the means and who think if they just pay a little more than the going rate, they'll definitely have no problems. When enough people do that, suddenly the higher amount becomes the new going rate. And so on and so on, until you have astronomical inflation. The soldiers begin to demand obscene amounts. It's untenable."

The colonel returns to his seat on the couch. He waves at the boxes of folders littering the room.

"That's what you have here," he says. "Inflation. Remember, a few years ago, when it was enough for them to say that the secret police had sent them a threatening letter or two, that a big man in dark glasses had looked at them funny when they were crossing the street? Now the going rate for suffering is higher. Now everyone has to claim they've been raped, tortured, their whole family wiped out, down to the pet dogs and the goldfish. Pretty soon they'll come to you claiming they're already dead. It's untenable, Madame El Ward. It can't go on like this."

"They don't deserve to suffer whatever grudges you still hold," Madame El Ward said. "This isn't a war zone, Dimitri."

"And it isn't hell either," the colonel says. "But if you do believe in hell, Nimra, then you must also believe no one ends up there who doesn't belong there."

The Colonel stands. He walks over to Madame El Ward. He places a hand on her shoulder. "Now," he says, "tell me where they went. Don't make me have you arrested for helping an unregistered illegal."

"The government changed that law," Madame El Ward says, swatting the colonel's hand away.

"Are you sure? Are you sure they haven't changed it back? Are you sure I couldn't make a single call to the ministry and have you thrown out of this place and replaced with one of my soldiers? Go join the Jesuits if you're looking for sainthood, but don't you dare get in the way of my work. That we are in a position to be fled to and not fled from is because we have systems, rules, proper ways of doing things. You want to see what it's like without systems? Hop on the next one of those boats that runs aground here and take it in the opposite direction."

"I've had enough of this," Madame El Ward says. "If you want to waste your time chasing a little boy around the island, that's your decision, but I can't help you."

Kethros sighs. "Yes you can, and you will," he replies. "And I never said it was a boy."

Chapter Fourteen

Before

A wailing foghorn shook the *Calypso*'s passengers awake. Mist hung in the air, a clouding thing. A few men yelled and scrambled about the upper deck looking for something, anything, to explain the sound.

"Stop moving, you idiots," shouted Mohamed. "You'll capsize the boat."

He pulled out his revolver, but in the darkness only the passengers closest to him saw it.

A knock to the head woke Amir. He had been resting against Umm Ibrahim, who was also asleep. But the foghorn blast caused her to flinch and in doing so she accidentally kneed the boy in his temple. Both woman and boy sat for an instant in a claustrophobic haze, their eyes open but feeble, the darkness of sleep taken over by the darkness of night.

"What is it?" Umm Ibrahim yelled at no one in particular. "Are we here? Are we here?"

"Calm down, lady," said someone nearby, barely visible from where Amir and Umm Ibrahim sat, but who Amir recognized by voice as Walid.

Just then a spine of white electricity appeared in the distance, perhaps a mile to the *Calypso*'s northwest. Slowly it came into focus—pole-mounted lights illuminating the deck of a huge freight ship. Lit this way and from the *Calypso*'s fog-blinkered view, the starboard side gave the vessel the appearance of a sparse floating city. With barely perceptible momentum it moved at an acute angle to the *Calypso*'s present direction, such that the two ships were likely to come within a few hundred feet of each other before they passed.

Some of the *Calypso*'s passengers rushed to the port side for a closer look at the freighter, but as soon as a few of them changed positions the old fishing boat began to tilt violently, such that many of their belongings dropped and tumbled. A scream let loose somewhere on the deck. Suddenly the passengers began fighting with one another, trying to pull back those who'd rushed to the port side. In the melee, the *Calypso* shook.

Amir held on to Umm Ibrahim's leg. He felt a sharp pain in his foot, as one of the other passengers ran over him in the darkness. As he leaned down to rub his toe, he noticed the ship had developed a heartbeat. A visible pulse rattled the deck floor, the wooden boards dancing ever so slightly, not in time with the passing waves but in some other chaotic measure. Amir lay his head closer to the floor. He heard muffled sounds of distress. From below, the passengers in the lower deck were screaming.

Through the small slit in the floorboards near where he sat, Amir could see them without seeing them. No more than a thin and rotting deck and a few feet of air separated him from the men and women whose panicked shouting shook the *Calypso*'s stomach. He felt the breath of them against his cheek, the heat of them, of bodies constrained and blinded. Still, in the black of night he could not see them, and when suddenly the tips of three fingers shot through the tear in the floorboards, Amir screamed and leapt up. A hand, bloody from where it scraped the wood and drew splinters, shot out from below, reaching for him. Elsewhere the passengers were hypnotized by the looming freighter, but Amir could only watch the bloodied hand, grasping at him and then drawing back into the darkness of the lower deck.

"Sit down, goddamn it," yelled Mohamed. Amid the shoving and shouting, he pushed his way to the middle of the boat, where Teddy stood at the wheel. Mohamed climbed atop the small roof of the wheelhouse. He stood head and shoulders above the rest of the passengers. He removed his pistol from his pocket and fired a shot into the air.

The silence that followed the blast was total. Everywhere along the top deck the men and women cowered.

"Listen very closely," Mohamed yelled. "If the people on that ship find you, one of two things will happen. Either they'll call the navy to come arrest you, or they'll sink you themselves. Whatever lies you've told yourselves about the kindness of Westerners, you need to forget that bullshit right now, because I promise you they will do anything they can to make sure you go back where you came from, or else die out here."

Mohamed waved his gun across the main deck in

a sweeping motion. "So here's what we're going to do. We're going to sit back down and we're going to stay very, very quiet until that ship passes. I don't want to hear a single one of you breathing."

The passengers complied. Now into the second night of voyage, they knew their places well enough to return to them instinctively, and even helped one another inch along the crowded deck. As they resettled in place, none spoke.

The freighter neared. Amir watched it breach the nighttime fog, its full size coming into view. It appeared to him as the largest thing he'd ever seen, larger than the sea itself. He tried to catch sight of any movement on the ship, any other sign of life, but the lights along the starboard side washed the deck. All Amir saw were stacks and stacks of shipping containers, tall as buildings.

Soon the passengers of the *Calypso* felt the displacing force of the ship. The waves rose and smacked the side of the fishing boat, knocking it side to side. The two vessels passed, the distance between them close enough to swim. And then they were behind it, watching the huge freighter slip back into the night.

For almost twenty minutes afterward, save for the monotonous wheeze of the engine below, the *Calypso* sailed without sound, no passenger on the top deck willing to be the first to speak, the silence spreading into the lower decks. Some of the men and women who'd been asleep earlier now began dozing off again. The waves settled.

In the quiet Amir became aware of a smell. It was faint under the weight of the salty Mediterranean air, secondary to the diesel stink and the all-encompassing smell of the sea itself, but it was there, and building. It was the smell of the passengers, the smell of human bodies in need of washing.

As the boat sputtered along, he sought to pass the time by building in his mind pictures of his mother and baby half brother, and then checking those images against the ones in the bell-shaped locket around his neck. But even when the clouds momentarily parted overhead and the moon swept across the deck, there was too little light to make out the tiny portraits. An inch away, the images were still as unreachable as the backs of clouds.

Even the sound that came to him from below, so hushed it barely registered, he at first took to be another half-remembered thing. Then he looked down and saw that it came through the gap in the floorboards.

Quiet Uncle called his name.

"Don't be afraid," he said. "It's going to be all right—we're almost there."

"Almost where?" Amir said, leaning down until his cheek once again touched the flooring. "Where are we going? What's happening?"

"I'm sorry," Quiet Uncle said. "I'm so sorry."

It was only then that a more intimate kind of fear replaced Amir's confusion. In all the years he'd known Quiet Uncle, he'd never heard from him a sincere apology.

"Please," Amir said, "tell me what this is."

"I was going to go away," Quiet Uncle said. "But only for a little while and only to see if it was true, if what they say . . . But I was always going to come back. No matter what, I would have come back. Do you understand?"

Amir said nothing. From below and absent light the voice seemed severed from its owner, a letter written but left unsigned.

"Say you understand," Quiet Uncle repeated. "Please say you understand."

Suddenly a sharp, shrill ringing tore through the upper deck. Amir and everyone around him jumped and once again wrestled impotently with the darkness in an attempt to make out the source of the sound. This time, though, it came from the boat itself.

"What the hell is it now?" yelled Mohamed.

"Sorry, sorry," came a reply in English from the wheelhouse. Teddy hit the alarm clock. "Shift change."

Many of the passengers on the upper deck shouted curses at the pilots as one handed over the wheel to the other. The commotion once again jump-started the boat's lower heartbeat. The passengers belowdecks began pounding the boards.

"Shut up—go back to sleep," Mohamed yelled, smacking the deck floor with his boot. "Everything's fine."

The alarm died down but now the deck buzzed with residual adrenaline. Whatever calm had been temporarily disturbed by the encounter with the passing freighter was now gone entirely. The back corner of the boat lit up as Walid turned on the flashlight and placed it in the lantern.

"Turn that off," Mohamed said. "People want to sleep."

"The people who still want to sleep are going to sleep, brother," Walid replied. "The people who can't sleep want light."

In the brightening Amir saw that the men and women

around him had . . . he could think of no word to express the change they'd undergone except *loosened*. Men who had come onto the boat far more formally dressed than this kind of trip required had by now undone the top buttons of their shirts and were using their jackets as blankets and pillows. A couple of the older women who'd arrived wearing hijabs had now either taken them off or turned them into high-riding scarves. So too was evident a melting of the communal posture—people slumped with their foreheads rested on their arms, their eyes cast down to the floor.

Even in the new light no one in Amir's corner of the boat felt the urge to speak. Maher, sitting in a cramped space almost directly below where the glass lantern hung, pulled his book out. No sooner had he flipped it open than Walid began peering over his shoulder.

"What are you reading, anyway?" he asked.

"The Book of Nicodemus," Maher replied. "From The Apocrypha."

"What the hell is that?"

"The books that didn't make the Bible."

"You want to know something?" Mohamed asked.

"Not really," Maher replied.

Mohamed continued on. "I've done enough of these trips now to get to know you people pretty well," he said. "I can read your future. I can do it by your clothing, by your game plans, what you say you're going to do when you get over there. But you want to know what the most accurate predictor is? Your belongings, the things you bring with you. And I'm sorry to say, brother, the ones who bring books never make it. They get eaten alive."

Kamal, who'd by now also given up on sleeping, sighed. "So you're a researcher now? You know all that from spending a couple of days with people on a boat?"

"No," Mohamed replied. "I know it from afterward too—from when you people call us up asking for help, because you had no idea what you were doing. You thought away was enough. But it's not. It never is."

"Why did you start doing this?" Kamal said. "You'll drown just like the rest of us if this piece of shit goes under. There's other ways to make a living."

"No there aren't." Mohamed pointed behind him, which he intended and all around him understood to be south, the city and the country and the world they'd left, although now there was no telling direction, no telling the places from the emptiness between them. "You know full well that where we come from whatever you end up doing is the only thing you could have ever ended up doing."

He turned to Maher. "That's how I know you won't make it: you carry stories around. You've got a storybook idea about how it'll end up, you've got a storybook view of the world."

Maher shrugged. "Books are good for the soul," he said. "Books will ween you off cruelty."

"And what will you be left with then?" Mohamed asked.

Amir sat back against the railing, a dull pain in his midsection. He turned and tugged slightly on the end of Umm Ibrahim's niqab.

"What is it, baby?" Umm Ibrahim said.

"I need to pee," Amir whispered.

Umm Ibrahim looked around the deck. "You can't hold it?" she asked.

Amir shook his head.

"All right," Umm Ibrahim said. She stood, wobbling a little as she sought to keep her balance. Awkwardly she shifted around so that she was now standing behind Amir, and Amir faced the railing, overlooking the sea. In the cramped confines of the deck a few neighboring passengers complained as the woman and the boy moved, but Umm Ibrahim ignored them.

"Go ahead," she told Amir. "Make sure you get it all in the water, not the boat."

"I can't go," Amir said, pointing to the passengers around him, who seemed utterly uninterested in this small spectacle but stared at him anyway because there was nothing else to look at.

Umm Ibrahim sighed. She turned and yelled at Walid.

"Hey, you. Give me your jacket."

"Huh?"

"Your jacket, your jacket. I need it to cover the boy up. He has to go to the bathroom."

"So let him go," Walid replied. "Who the hell cares what he does?"

"Have some decency," Umm Ibrahim said. "He's a little boy."

"So what? Everyone else on this boat has been pissing without covering up."

Walid pointed at the large orange life jacket in which Amir was encased. "He's dressed like a man, isn't he? Let him piss like a man."

Umm Ibrahim turned to Mohamed. "You want this night to go smoothly?" she said.

Mohamed raised his hands in a calming gesture. "Give her the damn jacket," he said to Walid. "It's just for a minute. Come on, be the bigger man."

"Fine," Walid said. He pulled the crumpled suit jacket from behind his head and threw it at Umm Ibrahim. It came unfurled midair and floated to rest on the floor midway along the deck between them. Three passengers handed it to one another until it reached Umm Ibrahim. She held it and stood directly behind Amir, covering his lower half in all directions but the one facing the sea.

"There," she said. "Go on."

"I can't reach," Amir said.

With the help of her immediate neighbor, Umm Ibrahim held Amir up from behind so he was elevated enough for his midsection to rise above the railing. Soon they'd succeeded in giving him the clearance he needed. Clumsily and unable to see what he was doing with the oversize life jacket riding all the way up to his temple, Amir finally relieved himself.

Even though he could barely hear the sprinkle of urine against the sea, there was something reassuring about the sound. Amir could not for the life of him understand why it was so soothing to hear this very faint dribble, which in a way resembled the sound of distant applause, but as the pain receded from his bladder, he felt so much lighter.

As he finished, a large wave collided with the *Calypso*'s starboard side. The boat rocked and the two passengers holding Amir momentarily lost their grip. He felt himself tipping forward, as though readying to take flight into the water. He screamed.

Then Umm Ibrahim caught him, pulling him back onto the deck. The two stumbled backward, knocking into a handful of others and violently displacing almost all the passengers in the back corner of the boat—all of whom, having watched the entirety of this performance, saw clearly the last of Amir's urine land not in the open sea but all over Walid's jacket.

Both woman and boy got up. Embarrassed, Amir quickly pulled his shorts back up and retreated to his corner of the deck. Umm Ibrahim stood up, calmly wrung the jacket out and dropped it in front of Walid.

"It got a little on it," she said. "Sorry."

Walid picked the jacket up with his thumb and forefinger. He stared at it, and then at the passengers around him, who didn't try very hard to contain their laughter.

"Just be grateful he wasn't shitting," said Mohamed.

"To hell with you," Walid said. "To hell with all of you." He turned and with great violence threw the jacket off the boat and into the sea.

Walid sat back in his corner. As the laughter died down, he stared at Amir. The boy hid his face behind his life jacket and the side of Umm Ibrahim's niqab but the man would not look away.

"Don't worry about it, baby," Umm Ibrahim whispered, petting Amir's head. "He won't do anything."

Amir looked upward. "Do you have any more apple slices?" he asked.

"I think they're all gone, but let me see," Umm Ibrahim said. She reached into her purse and rummaged around. She retrieved a mandarin, peeled it and handed half to Amir.

"Thank you," Amir said.

Quietly and unnoticed, he lowered his hand and slipped the fruit through the crack in the floorboard. Below, unseen, a hand brushed his and took it.

Chapter Fifteen

After

Around the back of the gymnasium, away from the main entrance, the guard instructs Vänna and Amir to walk quickly with their heads down. "Don't stop," he says. "Don't stare."

Vänna does as she's told and Amir mimics her, their eyes on the dirt road as they walk out of the facility. As the children leave, the refugees peer from their small, tattered tents to watch because this is what they have become: watchers, honed by captivity into seasoned observers of incremental change. But if any of them sense something odd about the small boy leaving the makeshift pen, none speak up.

Outside, the day is ending. The sun begins to disappear behind the middle-island mountains, where, Vänna learned as a small child, God Himself was born. The children cross a two-lane road and then a dirt field that ends at a hill overlooking the Hotel Xenios. Whenever the wind picks up it lifts the dust; soon Amir's legs are coated. By the time they reach the peak of the rolling hill, the sea spread out before them all along the eastern shore, both children are breathing hard.

Vänna looks to the south; she sees her house about a mile away. The lights are on, both floors radiating a warm yellow, soft against the dusk. Many nights, while out bird-watching or walking along the hilly footpaths, she's seen her home this way. It never ceases to amaze her how beautiful a place could look when seen from the right distance, in the right light.

Now she sees the same jeeps from earlier in the day coming up the road. They turn onto her parents' driveway and come to a stop. The soldiers disembark and, by the size of him, Vänna can tell Colonel Kethros is among them.

His soldiers wait outside; he enters.

They've been friends since college, he and her mother, and sometimes he drops by for a visit unannounced. She is someone else around him—not always happier, but more open to happiness, less indifferent. Vänna imagines this temporary variation of her is close to what she must have been like when she was younger. Sometimes when he visits, the two of them sit in the backyard by the empty pool and reminisce about college. Sometimes Vänna sits with Dadge, the sheepdog, in the pen by the side of the house and listens, and when she does, she hears Kethros talking to someone else entirely, a buoyant stranger with an easy, cackling laugh, and she hates herself for how much she wishes she had that stranger for a mother.

But she knows in her gut this isn't one of those visits. She can't shake the certainty that the colonel has discovered what she's done. It comes as no surprise to her. There's no use trying to hide anything on an island so small, a place where the people all know one another and take comfort in the knowing. No sooner does a secret come to life here than it becomes a barterer's currency. The colonel has discovered what she's done and now he's come to tell her parents.

For a second Vänna entertains the thought that maybe her father has spent the whole afternoon at the bottom of the bottle, and worked his way to that aggressive, sloppy drunkenness she associates with the foreign tourists. She wonders what he'll do, in that state, when Colonel Kethros walks into his home with news that his daughter has committed a crime, harbored and abetted an illegal, in violation not only of the law, but of something that predates and supersedes the law—something that lives in the history of her blood and the skin that encases her.

She hopes, in this impossible imagining, that her father stands up for her. She hopes he gets angry, maybe even throws a punch or two, taps into that dark chemical in the brain that turns insecure, slighted men to wrecking balls.

Of course there would never be any fighting, her father quickly pinned and pacified, punished for venturing to the visceral world where men like the colonel feel most comfortable. She can see it clearly, and can see just as clearly that if her father were ever so foolish as to try such a thing, it wouldn't be in defense of his daughter, but in defense of himself—of that sliver of pride that told him the finely uniformed man who so often paid visits to his home was not a man but a grotesque mirror in which he saw, obscenely magnified, every aspect in which he knew himself to be deficient.

It doesn't last long. A few minutes after he walks inside, Kethros leaves the home and the jeeps drive away. But only one of them continues up the road. The other remains parked on the shoulder a few feet away from the Hermeses' place, lights off.

As the other truck passes the hillside on the road below, Vänna instinctively drops down to her hands and knees, even though there's no chance anyone in the car can see the peak. She reaches back and brings Amir close to her, the two of them partially obscured among the brush. They remain this way until the jeep is gone.

Eventually, she knows there will be no hiding. Eventually they'll find her—either as she and the boy trek to the northeastern end of the island or afterward, on her way back home after delivering the boy to the ferryman, as Madame El Ward asked. This too she can see clearly: the way they'd drive her in silence back to her home, her mother waiting in the driveway, the look on her face not of disappointment, not even anger, but disgust.

There's no going home now, she thinks. Not until the child is delivered.

Vänna turns away from her home. She finds the boy looking eastward at the lights of the seaside hotel.

The Xenios, a sprawling modern cube of a building that hovers at the edge of the cliffside on the eastern shore, is alight with a neat trim of blue and white neon. Beyond the sleep-gum forest the children can see a series of interconnected swimming pools, shaped like elliptic doodles and joined by arching wooden footbridges. The underwater lights turn the pools a twinkling emerald. The day is ending and the tourists are leaving the beachfront; soon it will be quiet.

She knows by heart the route to the hotel, a winding footpath from the peak of the hill down to the poolside gardens, and she knows there exists a second craggy route over the coastal rocks that leads northward from the hotel grounds to the lighthouse, the place where Madame El Ward said the ferryman would be. That path, which is not a path at all, but the kind of secret go-between that exists almost exclusively on the treasure maps of children's minds, rarely sees any foot traffic. It veers well away from the main roads.

Vänna holds out her hand; Amir takes it. She leads him cautiously between the ferns and bushes but Amir moves ahead and pulls at her hand to go faster. Before long, gravity takes them; the children race toward the hotel grounds, gaining speed.

"*Yallah, yallah!*" Amir yells. The word is foreign to Vänna's ears but its meaning clear—it speaks of restlessness, movement. That she understands what the boy means on some instinctual level doesn't surprise Vänna, nor does the subconscious realization in that moment that it is natural for certain words to be subject to universal understanding—that, following its phrases for greeting and introduction, every culture's first linguistic export should be the directive *Let's go.*

With Amir egging her on to run faster, Vänna gives

up on following the thin dirt path. Soon the children are flying straight downhill, floating over the untouched ground between the switchbacks, laughing and dangerous with momentum.

The hill ends abruptly, giving way to a small patch of manicured grass at the edge of the hotel grounds. When Amir hits the grass his foot catches in the soil and he trips and tumbles forward. He lets out a little yelp, but is back on his feet before Vänna can get to him.

"No problem, no problem," he says in broken English as she looks him over.

Brushing the grass and soil from Amir's limbs, Vänna notices a reddening rash on his inner thighs. She guesses it's been caused by his clothes, made rough by the sea and needing to be washed, or better yet, discarded. Up close she can tell he has gone too long without bathing, though from her experience all boys to some extent smell unwashed.

Beyond a small gate circling the hotel's pool area, Vänna and Amir see a group of three kids at play. They're a little taller and broader than Amir but, she guesses, probably a year or two younger, strangely domineering over the physical space they occupy.

From a balustrade overlooking the pool area a woman dressed in a bright-red sarong calls for the three children to come upstairs. Begrudgingly, they pack their toys and water wings and towels. They climb the outdoor staircase that leads to a vast caramel-tiled patio—the cliffside balcony of the hotel's penthouse suite.

At the top of the stairs one of the children leaves his shirt hanging off the edge of the concrete railing.

Vänna waits until the children are out of sight, then she follows, Amir close behind her.

"Let's get you some new clothes," she says.

Vänna and Amir climb the concrete stairs, soundlessly and with great caution. At the top they see a group of tourists sitting on folding chairs and hammocks at the far side of the patio. There's perhaps a dozen in all, three adult couples, the rest children of all ages. They gather, popcorn in hand, in front of a large white projector screen, readying to watch a movie.

Vänna and Amir duck behind the low concrete wall at the top of the stairs, spying. To their left, beyond the patio's eastern railing, the land drops sharply along a sheer cliff to the beachside, offering an unobstructed view of the sea. To their right, two sets of floor-to-ceiling windows separate the interior of the penthouse suite from the veranda.

Vänna reaches up and grabs the shirt left behind by one of the tourists' children. Unfurling it, she sees it's too large for Amir's frame and, worse, soaked. She tosses it back over the railing.

On the other side of the balcony, the projector begins to whirr. The opening titles of an old black-and-white movie Vänna doesn't recognize appear on the white projector screen—a sweeping Orientalist orchestral, a neatly bordered map of Africa and Arabia. The tourists sit on their outdoor reclining chairs, watching, oblivious to the surrounding world.

Vänna turns to Amir. In clumsy pantomime she tries to explain that she plans to sneak into the tourists' suite, and that he should stay put and play the part of lookout, keeping an eye and alerting her by waving should one of the tourists decide to return to the hotel room. The boy stares at her, and it doesn't appear he understands a single thing she's trying to say.

"Got it?" she asks, giving him a thumbs-up. He nods and responds in kind.

Vänna sneaks around the edge of the railing and onto the balcony. She moves quickly, still in a half crouch, toward the sliding glass door that leads from the balcony to one of the bedrooms. She slides the door open and slips inside.

It's a vast room of inoffensive luxury. On a clean white double dresser stands a clean white lamp and under the lamp's clean white glow it is difficult to tell where one accessory begins and the other ends.

Vänna opens the dresser drawers. In the first she finds underwear and in the second Bermuda shorts and shirts. In the third she finds children's clothes.

She pulls out a pair of boys' underwear and a pair of socks and the topmost shirt from a neatly folded pile. But before she can rummage for a pair of pants or shorts, she turns to check on Amir through the window and sees him standing by the edge of the balcony steps, his eyes wide with alarm. He waves at the far end of the balcony and then at her.

Vänna drops to the ground. She crawls under the bed and lies perfectly still, watching the bottom edge of the sliding glass door, waiting. It seems in that moment incomprehensible to her that anyone within earshot would not immediately be alerted to her presence by the sound her heartbeat makes against the floor. She tries to hold her breath.

A minute passes, then another. Finally Vänna begins to inch forward on her stomach, poking her head out from under the bed. She listens for the sound of footsteps from the other side of the room, in case someone has walked in from the suite's living area. She hears nothing. Carefully she lifts herself up and out from under the bed. She looks at the balcony, entirely empty but for the family sitting at the far end, who appear not to have moved at all. She looks back at the edge of the staircase on the other side of the balcony. She sees Amir pointing at her and laughing.

Vänna stands up and marches out of the hotel room, pushing the glass door open without care of being caught. She walks over to Amir and grabs him by the shoulder and pulls him around the edge of the railing and down the stairs.

When they reach the bottom and are safely out of view, she shakes him by both shoulders.

"Are you kidding?" she yells. "You want to get caught? Is that what you want?"

But the boy can't stop giggling and in his sheer joy at having tricked her there is something of a contagion.

"It's not funny," Vänna says, smiling. "Let's go, before someone calls the police."

She takes him by the hand. They walk down a deserted outdoor corridor, past the doors of the pool-facing hotel rooms along the ground floor.

As they near the end of the corridor, their path is suddenly obstructed by a housekeeping cart turning the corner. They find themselves face-to-face with a member of the Hotel Xenios staff, a middle-aged woman dressed in the hotel's blue and white housekeeping uniform. All three freeze.

The housekeeper eyes both boy and girl, uncertain. In the way she looks at him, Amir senses that this woman is one of the people whose approval was of such importance to the men and women he traveled with on the *Calypso*. And on the tail of this thought comes another realization—that he is in possession of the pass phrase to be used in exactly such a situation. He takes a step toward the housekeeper and recites in broken English the words he's memorized phonetically from days of repeated hearings.

"Hello," he says. "I am pregnant. I will have baby on April twenty-eight. I need hospital and doctor to have safe baby. Please help."

The woman looks at the boy. She says nothing.

Amir, unsure whether he's mispronounced something, begins once more to recite the sounds he memorized. This time, Vänna puts her hand against his chest. She turns to the housekeeper.

"Please don't tell," she says.

A wave of recognition washes over the housekeeper's face.

"From this morning?" she asks Vänna, but doesn't wait for the girl to answer. Instead, she begins rummaging around her cart, then suddenly she stops.

"Don't go anywhere," she says.

Before Vänna can reply, the housekeeper opens the door to one of the ground-floor rooms and disappears inside. She emerges with a handful of minibar provisions—cookies, chips, cashews, a bottle of water. She unfolds one of the pillowcases in her cart and begins stuffing it with these things and then others—small bottles of shampoo and conditioner, bars of soap, a towel, pillow mints.

And then she stops again, as though arrested by some violent passing force. She steps around her cart and closes in on Amir, so suddenly and with such mysterious but obvious purpose that the boy instinctively takes a step backward. She kneels down and inspects him closely, her hand cupped under his chin.

Without looking at her, the housekeeper speaks to Vänna. She points north, beyond the pool to the small hotel beachfront in the distance.

"There's an outdoor shower over there," she says. "Do you have something else for him to wear?"

"Yes," Vänna says.

"Then go. It'll be empty now."

The housekeeper grabs the stuffed pillowcase and passes it to Vänna, all the while still staring at the boy. In this way she remains, seemingly on the verge of saying something but made entirely of silence.

Vänna takes Amir's hand and begins to lead him away. They take only a few steps before the housekeeper says, "Wait."

Vänna stops. The housekeeper kneels down beside the door of one of the hotel rooms and picks up a covered plate, the remnants of some guest's room-service order. She hands it to Vänna, who lifts the metal cover to find a mostly uneaten lamb roast.

"These people . . ." the housekeeper says, looking back at the row of hotel room doors. She trails off.

"Thank you," Vänna says.

Soon they arrive at All Saints' Beach, a small seafront that once was a public space but is now Xenios property, all the way up to the ancient ruins farther inland. In the fading dusklight the beach is empty, the only trace of tourists a few abandoned hotel towels and sunscreen bottles. The water glistens, still and clear as glass.

Always, the tourists rave about the clarity of the water. Here on the island, where the economy runs on foreigners' money, there exists an obsession with the transparency of it, the way one can stand on a nearby cliffside and, looking down, view plainly everything that lives beneath the surface. The tourists seem to prize this above all else; it doesn't much matter what lines the seabed, so long as they can see it from a distance, decipher it with their eyes rather than the soles of their feet.

Vänna leads Amir to the northern corner of the beach, where the hotel has installed a set of outdoor showers. She hangs the stolen clothes on the side of a small, weathered skiff that sits near the showers and may have once been used for fishing but is now purely decorative. She sets down a small bottle of shampoo and a bar of soap on the tiled shower stall floor.

"Go on," she says, pointing to Amir and then the shower, making a scrubbing motion with her hand.

Amir shakes his head. He responds with a hand motion of his own, a pantomime that resembles a hand unscrewing a lightbulb.

"What?" Vänna says.

With more agitation Amir points at Vänna and makes the same motion again, until she finally understands. She turns around, her back to the shower.

A few seconds later she hears the water run, a yelp as the coldness of it touches the boy's skin. She stands facing the sea and waits.

In a while the water stops running. She hears the sounds of him changing into his stolen clothes and then she feels a tap on her shoulder. The shirt she grabbed appears to be a sports jersey of sorts, white with an offensively cartoonish, red-faced caricature of a man on the chest, and though Vänna has no idea what team or sport this illustration represents, it is plain to see that the jersey is too large. Amir wears it like a full-length dress.

"Looks good," Vänna says, smiling.

In her periphery, she catches the sweep of a distant flashlight. She turns to find a security guard from the Hotel Xenios patrolling the pool area adjacent to the other side of the beach. He moves slowly and without purpose, checking his phone as he walks.

"*Yallah, yallah,*" says Amir, tugging on Vänna's arm.

"All right, *yallah,*" Vänna repeats. They hurry northward, past the end of the beach and along the uneven land where the rocks dive headlong into the sea, the outer rim of the island.

Soon they come upon a small cave, set far enough back from the water that Vänna assumes no change in tide will flood it. She leads Amir beneath the overhanging rocks and sets down her pillowcase and the plate of hotel food and the child's backpack Madame El Ward gave her.

"Here is good enough," she says.

They sit awhile in the shallow belly of the cave. They observe each other. In time the immediacy of adventure leaves them and in a way they become the strangers they never had a chance to be, discovering each other anew.

She notices for the first time that his hair is naturally curly, and, washed now of the residual grime of the sea, he looks younger, more luminous. His skin is darker than hers; it matches the shade she subconsciously associates not with a country or an ethnicity but with the entire middle belt of the Earth. He looks like an islander.

She smiles at him. He smiles back.

Suddenly Vänna remembers the books Madame El Ward gave her. She opens the small backpack and retrieves them. She starts with one of the translation books. It was published a year earlier by one of the volunteer-run resettlement groups and is intended for children. She flips through the pages casually, past cartoon animals whose speech bubbles bear greetings and simple declarations in a dozen different languages— some she speaks, some she can guess at, some she can't begin to decipher.

On a page she finds a map of the sea that surrounds them. She points to her island and looks at the boy.

"This is us," she says, pointing at the both of them.

Amir observes the map. He points to a place on the other side of the sea.

Vänna nods. Looking up at him, she notices for the

first time around the boy's neck a gold bell-shaped necklace. In the action of the day its shell-clasp has come loose and it hangs open now, baring its insides. She looks at the two photos within, one she assumes is of the boy's mother and the other of him as a baby.

"Did you come here alone?" she asks, but the boy doesn't understand.

Vänna thinks a moment, then points to the necklace. To her surprise, the boy takes it off from around his neck and hands it to her.

Delicately Vänna sets the open locket onto the page, such that the picture of the woman sits atop the land on one side of the sea. Then she slowly moves the locket across the blue on the page, until in an inch or two the woman's photo arrives on the island.

She watches the boy follow the journey in miniature. He looks up at her. He shakes his head. He begins to cry softly.

"I'm so sorry," Vänna says. She pulls him close. She tries to think of some way to cross the gap of language and reach him, to offer some comfort.

"Look, look," she says. With her arm still around him she leans the two of them forward such that they can see out the mouth of the cave. She points northward, to the end of the island.

"When we get there, there's a man who'll . . ." She stops. She picks up the phrase book and the necklace and moves the pictures back in the other direction. The boy smiles.

"It'll be okay, David," she says.

For a second Amir, who has forgotten the fake name

he'd given her earlier in the day, stares in confusion. Then he remembers.

"No David, no David," he says. "Amir."

Vänna nods. She reaches out and shakes the boy's hand.

"Hello, Amir," she says. "I'm still Vänna."

She hands the necklace back, then takes the plate the hotel housekeeper gave her and sets it between them, using the open translation book as a place mat. They sit in silence eating the guests' leftovers, Amir inhaling a mostly uneaten, overcooked roast, Vänna picking at the garnish, a few small stalks of watercress.

A few minutes later, she stands up. She motions for Amir to keep eating, then walks out of the cave and back down the shoreline toward All Saints' Beach. She returns carrying a pair of the hotel's beach-chair cushions. She sets them down side by side in the cave, then she lies down and kicks the sandals off her feet and wipes the sand from her skirt. She looks at Amir and pats the other empty cushion.

They lie down beside each other. The cushions are narrow; they are forced close together, and in that closeness she can feel the rise and fall of his breathing. Night falls, silence settles alongside it, and the children sleep.

Chapter Sixteen

Before

"And what's so bad about America?" Kamal asked.

"You poor, deluded man," said Mohamed. "Where to begin, where to begin?"

For hours the migrants in Amir's corner of the boat had passed the time this way, talking about their destinations, the places where they hoped to settle one day. Like the boat in which they traveled, the conversation seemed to take no direction at all, in this moment a heated debate about the inhumanity of the Dublin agreement, in the next an exchange of advice on how to best avoid the suspicion of the police officers who patrolled the train from Copenhagen to Malmö, how to best imitate a Westerner. And preoccupied with conversation, the men and women were able to keep from thinking about the journey, about their depleting supply of food and water and the smell of unwashed skin, which had now overpowered that of the diesel fumes. So they talked, and their talk filled the emptiness that surrounded them.

"How do you even plan to get to America?" Mohamed said.

"I'll figure it out," Kamal said. "I have a cousin there."

Mohamed finished a small plastic bottle of water and tossed it overboard. "There are three things you need to know about America," he said. "First, everyone there is racist, especially the ones who tell you they're not. Second, they're terrified of sex. And third, no matter the crime, they'll always find themselves innocent."

Kamal stared at Mohamed, incredulous. "What the hell are you talking about?" he said. "You come from our part of the world and you want to tell me Americans are terrified of sex? Americans are more comfortable with sex than anyone."

"No," Mohamed replied. "They're comfortable with violence, not sex. Sometimes they just get the two confused."

Mohamed turned to Maher. "Hey, English professor, tell me I'm wrong."

"Which America?" Maher replied. "There's lots of countries inside that country."

"The America that gets to decide what to do with people like us."

"No," Maher said. "You're not wrong."

Kamal waved Mohamed off. "What do I care what they're terrified of, anyway? And you want to throw stones, look at this boat."

Kamal pointed to the floor, below which the lower galleys hummed. "Look at the skin color of the people up here and look at the skin color of the people down there and tell me we're any better."

Mohamed shook his head. "That has nothing to do with the color of anyone's skin. There's a price to sit up here and there's a price to sit down there. If any of those Africans had enough money to be sitting in the top deck, that's where they'd be. This is about business, not race."

"Keep telling yourself that," Kamal replied.

Amir leaned against Umm Ibrahim's knee, cramped and in pain. Earlier, the sea had kicked up and sent the boat rocking. Umm Ibrahim, her little vial of lemon juice long empty and with nothing else to keep the nausea at bay, had succumbed to seasickness. Barely able to lift her niqab's face covering in time, she threw up a thin stream of fluid off the side of the boat. The passengers against whom she'd been pressed tried to move out of her way, and all succeeded but for Amir. Before he knew what had happened, the back of his shirt and life jacket were soggy with vomit.

"I'm sorry, baby," Umm Ibrahim said between gulping breaths, trying to regain her equilibrium.

Amir recoiled. He unzipped his life jacket and took off his shirt and under the gaze of all around him he stared at the thin yellow liquid that stained both.

Umm Ibrahim pointed to the men who sat near her. "Someone give him a shirt to wear," she said.

None of the men responded. In their silent reticence was evident the reality that somewhere along the journey they'd passed the point where human goodness gave way to the calculus of survival. Passengers who a day earlier had shared with Amir a sip of canned orange juice or a bag of sunflower seeds or a bite of stone-hard baklava, or had simply smiled in his direction, now looked straight through him.

"What pathetic men you are," Umm Ibrahim said.

"Lady, calm down," said Walid. "It's hot out. Let him sit without a shirt—it won't kill him."

"Shut up," Umm Ibrahim said. She snapped her fingers in the direction of Maher, who sat in silence reading his book. "You," she said. "Hand me that rope."

Maher snapped out of his hypnosis and looked around him. On the deck near where he sat was a line of coiled rope, fraying but thick.

"This?" Maher asked.

"Yes, this," Umm Ibrahim replied. "Don't stare at me like that. Let's go, let's go."

"Would you just sit back in your place and calm down?" Walid said. "Enough with this . . ."

"Tell me to calm down again," Umm Ibrahim said. "Tell me to calm down again, see what happens."

Maher struggled to lift the rope, which required the assistance of three other passengers, who sat on parts of it. Finally, he managed to pass one end to Umm Ibrahim, who laced it through the arms of Amir's jacket and shirt, then tied it in a double-overhand. She leaned over the railing and dipped the makeshift clothesline into the water.

Amir stood and watched, as did a few of his seatmates, none of whom, caught up in the strangeness of Umm Ibrahim's ad hoc washing, noticed that the life jacket remained afloat only for an instant before sinking below the surface.

A moment later Umm Ibrahim pulled the line. She set

the jacket and the shirt on the edge of the railing behind her and looped the rope through a hook to pin the clothing in place.

"It'll be dry soon," she told Amir. "Good as new."

Amir sat back down on the deck between Umm Ibrahim's feet. Soon the passengers ignored him again, and he felt less self-conscious of his skin.

He remembered watching his mother throw up, in the months before his half brother was born—the violence of it, the way the muscles inside her seemed to seize, a strange electricity working its way through her as she leaned against the bowl. Whenever he saw her this way she was always careful afterward to tell him that it was natural, but it never looked natural. Or if it was natural, it was the workings of a nature bereft of mercy, bereft of grace.

Once he'd heard his mother talking with the other immigrant women who lived in the neighborhood. The conversation turned to childbirth, one of the women due in a few weeks and deeply anxious about how the local doctors would treat her and her newborn.

Babies are resilient, Amir's mother said—it's a medical fact that babies are born knowing the basics of survival; should a woman give birth alone in the forest and pass out during, the child would come out knowing how to crawl, how to reach its mother's breast, how to hold on.

Amir thought back to this conversation now, and, feeling the curve of Umm Ibrahim's belly against the back of his head, wondered if there was any truth to what his mother had said. Would a child born in the forest really come out knowing how to crawl? It seemed entirely impossible, as much the stuff of fantasy as Umm Ibrahim giving birth out here and the child born knowing how to swim.

In time the swaying boat lulled him into a nap. When he woke, the sun had set but not before leaving its mark on him. His back burned. He reached over and asked Umm Ibrahim to give him his clothes. He put them on— his shirt had dried but the life jacket was still soaked. In the cooling night he leaned against Umm Ibrahim's knee and leached warmth.

Chapter Seventeen

After

D o you even recognize your country anymore?
Be honest—do you?"

The interviewer, eager to move on, taps
her pen and begins to ask the next question.

"No, wait," the man says. "Tell me this, tell me this:
Why do they all have phones? If they're all so poor, why
do they have phones?"

"I don't know why they have phones," the interviewer
replies.

"And another thing—why do these women keep asking for birth control pills? Half of them claim their hus-
bands were killed by the secret police or whatever—after
all, that's what brought them here, isn't it?—but the people who run the immigration facilities tell me they keep
asking for birth control pills. Why, why?"

"I don't know why they keep asking for birth control
pills," the interviewer replies.

Colonel Kethros watches. He recognizes the man
being interviewed on TV as a representative of one of
the nationalist parties, which have been making seri-

ous inroads over the past two years, capitalizing on the migrant crisis and the humiliating economic malaise.

"Do we have to listen to this nonsense?" says the colonel's companion, Lina Eliades, an administrator with the Ministry of Migration Policy, whose job over the last year has entailed chasing the geographic whims of the migrant passage. She spends most of her time traveling from the site of one boat landing to the other—liaising with local officials, standardizing the myriad forms used by different municipalities to count the living, taking guesses at the number of dead. She has known Colonel Kethros since grade school; they make time to meet whenever work brings Lina back to the island.

"He's putting on a performance," Kethros says, pointing the remote at the television.

"Of course he's putting on a performance," Lina replies. "That's the whole point."

The colonel shakes his head. "But it doesn't mean he's wrong."

Low clouds mute the morning sun. Across the street from where Lina and the colonel sit at a small roadside coffee shop, the grounds of the Hotel Xenios appear a ghost town compared to the previous day. The journalists are all gone; news arrives that another boat has washed up on one of the nearby islands where a popular movie festival is under way, and the visuals of such a landing—the chance to catch movie stars and migrants in a single shot—are too good to pass up. The soldiers and emergency workers and representatives from the coroner's office have finished clearing away the bodies; likely they are sitting now in cold storage in the city morgue, subject to a set of death rites that, even now, after so many similar deaths, are still ad hoc and carried out by the state with endless reluctance.

The colonel turns to his friend. "Tell me what you know about the next one," he says.

"What next one?" Lina replies.

"Don't play games, Lina. We all hear the same radio chatter."

Lina sighs. "I don't know," she says. "A party boat reported it, said it looked like a large life raft."

"Different from the one that just washed up next door?"

"Probably. We have reports of three different ones, or maybe the same."

"Headed this way?"

"Who can say? They don't steer those things—they just float."

The colonel finishes his coffee and lights a cigarette. "Nothing for months, and now two in two days."

"Relax," Lina says. "You're starting to sound like my bosses."

The colonel points south, beyond the hotel grounds to the sea and what lies on the other side of the sea. "Your bosses are letting them colonize us," he says.

"You're getting melodramatic in your old age," Lina replies. "It's not a colonization, it's just a bunch of people on boats."

"Every colonization is just a bunch of people on boats," the colonel says.

He looks across the street, where his soldiers loiter around their trucks, waiting on him. They are new recruits and much too young, the colonel believes, to be assigned any real responsibility. Elias and Alexander, the twins, work well together, and Andreas, who was born on the eastern side of the island, is at least good for local knowledge. But the fourth of the bunch, Nicholas, is much too soft, too bookish, clearly unsuited for military life.

In a way they all are. At times they carry out his orders silently and robotically. Other times, when he is in a good mood and behaves in a friendlier manner with them, they become too familiar, and soon start to bombard him with questions about his previous military experiences: what it was like to see the peace collapse, to work a slaughter field; whether he felt his lower leg come detached from his body in the moment the mine exploded; whether he ever killed. In times like these the colonel feels a great and sullen rage overtake him—not at the boys themselves, who behave the same way he did at their age, but at the fact that the end of his military career should have come to this: babysitting four little boys, running around from migrant ship to migrant ship, swatting at flies.

A couple of tourists walk barefoot across the street from the hotel grounds to the coffee shop. As they approach, Lina smiles and says, "Good morning." The tourists smile back politely and exchange greetings but quickly pay for their drinks and walk away, looking warily at the military pickup truck parked across the street and the four soldiers gathered around it.

"You're scaring the foreigners," Lina says.

The colonel chuckles. "The foreigners are scaring themselves."

Lina opens her briefcase and pulls out a plain paper folder. "So, do you have numbers for me?" she asks.

"One hundred and twenty, give or take," the colonel replies.

"Give or take . . ."

The colonel sighs. "What do you want from me, Lina?"

"Accurate numbers, Dimitri. Has anyone told you how to do your job out here? No, we leave you alone, we let you do whatever you think is best. The only thing we ask for is accurate numbers."

"One hundred and twenty-four."

"No unaccounted for?" Lina asks.

"You want me to dredge the seafloor?" the colonel replies.

"The government doesn't care about the seafloor, the government cares about the land. No unaccounted for on the island?"

The colonel says nothing. Lina repeats her question.

"No," Kethros replies. "No unaccounted for on the island."

"Thank you." Lina scribbles a few lines on the back of her folder and puts it back in her briefcase. "When you can, have someone from your office put it down in writing and send it over."

Kethros watches the tourists hurrying back to the hotel grounds. "Our mistake was getting into the nice business," he says.

"I'm sorry?"

"We thought tourism would be easy money—the sea is already here, the sand is already here, what's left but to be nice? What's easier than to be nice?"

Lina points to the Xenios. "A few hundred fishermen on this island who have nothing left to fish can still put food on the table because of the nice business."

The colonel shakes his head. "For now, maybe. But you can't bet your future on work that requires the coming together of people, not now, not with the world the way it is. The days of people coming together are ending; this is a time for coming apart."

Lina packs her papers. She says good-bye to the colonel and leaves in her small rented sedan to make her way back to the city, where she will spend the night waiting to hear where the latest migrant ghost ship has been sighted next, or if it's ever sighted again.

Alone in the roadside café, Kethros turns his attention back to the man on the television. The interview has become more heated, and now both journalist and politician are talking over each other. Then, almost in unison, both seem to become aware of this, of how it must look to their audience, and a tense calm returns to the proceedings.

"I want to ask you about the government's special provisions for underage asylum seekers," the interviewer says. "You've been a frequent and vocal critic of this policy."

"I have," the politician replies.

"You said it conveys weakness."

"I have."

"But we're talking about children," the interviewer

says. "Just recently we saw the now-infamous images of a child in one of the immigrant facilities—"

"That was last year."

"That was last month. Do you honestly think the state has no special obligations to that child?"

"It is not the responsibility of the state," the politician replies. "It is the responsibility of its parents, who chose to bring it on this kind of journey."

Colonel Kethros changes the channel. A replay of a soccer match takes the place of the interview. The colonel leans back in his chair. He closes his eyes.

Sometimes the small details of the nightmare change. Sometimes the mother and the father are different, but the child is always the same. Young, of indeterminate gender, and blond, which none of the other children in this place are. Sometimes the father slices a mango with a paring knife, the juice running down his forearms. Sometimes he hums an old folk song. Sometimes he is dead, his corpse propped up against a bale of straw, his wife slowly moving an emery board against his broken fingernails. But the boy is always the same—serene, his blank gray eyes fixed to a spot down the road.

The soldiers are patrolling the country road, and to pass the time they dream up torture. It's a game they play, a piece of communal black humor without physics or metaphysics. The point is to use no violence, but be as cruel as possible.

Pareen, the youngest of the peacekeepers, suggests finding out what a prisoner's mother used to cook him when he was a child, and then feeding him those meals every day in his cell, only with one key ingredient missing or altered each time. Kareem suggests a minor lobotomy, to remove all familiarity with sneezing, and then smearing pepper on the walls. Imagine, he says, how disoriented he'd be, how utterly terrified, every time.

When his turn comes, Kethros suggests putting the captive back in uniform, handing him a weapon, throwing him into the middle of a genocide and ordering him to do nothing, to simply sit on the sidelines and watch, helpless. The men stop talking, the game loses its fun.

One of the soldiers sees the child. Reflexively he removes some caramels from the pouch of his rucksack and throws them toward the side of the road. But the child does not move. He simply stares down the road, to the place where, moments later, the trap will spring.

Sometimes the earth opens up slowly. Sometimes Kethros feels the air rush outward, feels his rib cage compress and his lungs crumple, the lifting, the emptying of space. Sometimes it doesn't happen at all, sometimes the soldier ahead of him never reaches the place in the road to which the child's gaze is tethered. Sometimes, as in a dream about falling, Kethros wakes an instant before impact, drenched in sweat and grasping at nothing.

Kethros opens his eyes and jolts upright on his seat. He composes himself, sheds the aftertaste of the dream, just as Jonathan Hoff, who for the past year has served as the general manager of the Hotel Xenios, walks over from the hotel to see him.

"I need to speak with you, Colonel," Jonathan says. "Your soldiers won't help me."

"It's not my soldiers' job to help you, Jonathan," the colonel replies.

"The people you're supposed to be catching are causing our guests trouble."

"And which people are we supposed to be catching, exactly?"

Jonathan points in the general direction of the sea. "Those people," he says.

The colonel sighs. "Go away, Jonathan."

The hotel manager continues to plead, but quickly resigns himself to the colonel's indifference. He makes to leave. "What kind of person steals children's clothes?" he says as he walks away.

Colonel Kethros stands up.

"What did you say?"

Jonathan turns around. "The guests staying in our penthouse suite had their son's favorite shirt stolen. Where they come from, everyone sues everyone; they're threatening to take us to court."

"When did it happen?" the colonel asks.

"Sometime yesterday," Jonathan replies. "Last night, probably."

Colonel Kethros stands. He grabs Jonathan by the arm and walks him over to where the four soldiers stand by their truck.

"Show us exactly where it happened," the colonel says.

Chapter Eighteen

Before

What about you, Professor Maher?" Mohamed asked. "Where are you going?" Maher marked his place in his book with Kamal's forged identification card. He looked up.

"Wherever," he replied.

"That's the spirit," Mohamed said. He motioned to the rest of the men and women sitting nearby, speaking to no one in particular. "This is how you have to be if you want to survive over there," he said. "Flexible."

"Hey, Hajj, you got any more gum?" Kamal asked, addressing someone sitting opposite him on the deck, indistinguishable among the mass of bodies cramped together. Nobody answered.

"So what was it, then?" Mohamed said, returning to Maher. "The Israelis demolish your house, beat you at a checkpoint?"

"I don't care about the Israelis," said Maher.

"Yes you do," Mohamed replied. "People don't end up on boats like this unless their life depends on being somewhere or not being somewhere. If you really don't care where you end up, then you sure as hell have a good reason for leaving."

"I didn't," Maher said. "I just left."

Mohamed chuckled. "Real easygoing, this one," he said. "So you left for no reason, you have no destination. What is it you want then, brother?"

Maher shrugged. "I want to read books and be left alone," he said.

"Hey, Hajj, over here," Kamal shouted again, waving his hand. No one responded.

"This is why they don't take us seriously," Walid said, pointing his phone in Maher's direction. "Read books? Brother, learn a trade, learn computers."

"Why?" Maher replied.

"Because that's how we take the future from them," Walid said, animated now. "Look at Stockholm, look at Munich, look at New York—who's picking up the garbage, cleaning the toilets? Who's doing the work? Us. Who's doing the living? Them. But in ten, twenty years, we'll be the ones running the computers, the machines, the *infrastructure*, and they'll have nothing left but poems and stories."

"So they'll still do all the living," Maher replied, "and we'll still do all the work."

The men paused. Almost in unison, the ship's passengers felt a change in the weather. Light, almost imperceptible at first, snow began to fall.

"Great, just great," said Walid. "This is all we need."

"Relax," Mohamed replied. "It's not the end of the world."

Maher wiped a couple of wet flakes from his book. He

chuckled. "I don't suppose you have blankets for sale?" he asked Mohamed.

Mohamed smiled. "Friend, if the price is right, I'll fish you a blanket from the bottom of the sea."

"Something's wrong," Kamal said.

"No kidding," Walid replied. "That's the only thing that matters to these people." He pointed at Mohamed. "Money, money, money."

Mohamed opened his palm to the sky. He watched the snowflakes disintegrate against the heat of his skin. "You keep mistaking this for a charity," he said. He pointed to Kamal. "Ask your friend here, the economics dropout. We live under the invisible hand, not the invisible foot. This is a transaction, a business arrangement."

"Bullshit," Walid replied. "You promised a cruise ship, you promised meals. Why is it so hard for you to admit it: you lied to us."

"You lied to yourself," Mohamed said. "Did you really think there'd be a goddamn cruise ship waiting for you, because you saw it in the picture? Did you really think we'd feed you lobster for dinner every night? Brother, by the time we started lying to you, you'd already believed it."

"You're a thief," Walid said. "Dress it up however you want, but you're just another black-market hustler."

"That's exactly what I am," Mohamed replied. "And when you finally get over there to the promised land, and you see how those dignified, civilized Westerners treat you—when you find out what they expect of you is to live your whole life like a dog under their dinner table—I'll wait for you to come find me and apologize.

You think the black market is bad? Brother, wait till you see the white market."

"Wait a minute," Kamal said, this time loud enough that the conversation came to a halt. The passengers seated near the Egyptian turned to look in the direction where Kamal was squinting. It was the other side of the deck, port, where Amir and Umm Ibrahim were seated near a dozen others.

Kamal stood up. He began traversing the deck, eliciting complaints from the people over and around whom he stepped.

"Sit down," Mohamed said, but Kamal ignored him. He walked to the edge of the deck and knelt down close to an old man propped against the railing.

He was dressed in a thin white galabeya. He wore an embroidered, rounded skullcap on his head and it appeared at some point during the journey he had taken his socks off and used them instead as gloves. He sat motionless, his head lolling to one side

Kamal tapped the old man on the shoulder. "Hajj, Hajj," he said. The old man did not respond.

A kind of knowing spread among the nearby passengers, and some of them inched away. Kamal held the old man by one arm. He looked over to Mohamed.

"Goddamn it," Mohamed said. "Goddamn it."

Chapter Nineteen

After

Vänna rubs her eyes. In the morning light, through the porthole of the cave's mouth, the world seems inverted; she looks out at the sober-bright sea.

To the north, the coast becomes snakelike, thinning and curling around itself such that the island's northeast tip, the children's destination, is mostly hidden from view. Although Vänna knows the area around this beach like the back of her hand, the land to the northeast is largely foreign to her. Looking at it now, its wide hills of brush and rock rising and falling, rising and falling, it appears a fictional place, a stage-play setting fit for the myths and wild, ancient stories that saddle this island's history. And yet there's an emptiness, something missing. In stories these places were lined with thick forests and streams, the ocean wild and roaring. Here the hills are mostly bare, their bareness made more evident by the smattering of sleep-gum trees and decrepit stone dwellings and the silence of the water.

She twists slightly in place and hears her spine and

neck bones crackle. She eases away from where Amir lies, careful not to disturb him. In the night she thought she heard him moaning softly in his sleep, and when she tried to wrap her arm around him to comfort him, he let out a scream and wrestled her away. But the whole time, he never opened his eyes, never left sleep.

She stretches her legs to let the sunlight warm them, and watches as the indent of her body slowly disappears from the beach-chair cushion behind her. She watches the boy sleeping.

In time he starts to stir, and when he wakes and sees Vänna at the edge of the cave, his face contorts into a look of such total terror that for a moment Vänna thinks the soldiers are standing outside the cave behind her. But then he seems to remember her. He smiles sheepishly and waves hello.

Vänna waves back. She reaches into the pillowcase bag the housekeeper gave them the night before. Amir shuffles over and sits beside her. They spend a few silent minutes breakfasting on cookies and chocolate mints, the top halves of their bodies still hidden, their legs sticking out, warming.

Vänna points Amir's attention northward. Faint in the distance, atop a rocky outcropping that itself is invisible, stand the ruins of an ancient lighthouse. Only the very tip of the cupola and a leaning lightning rod can be seen from where the children sit.

It is, like the ruins lining so much of the coastline, secret with age. Over the centuries it has been used, disused, retrofitted, neglected, transformed to historical and tourist curiosity and, finally, ignored. No one on the island can say when it last served any meaningful purpose at all, the lantern room nothing more than an empty circular space where drunk teenagers occasionally congregate. But, even decrepit, it has held on to its first and foremost use: to be seen.

"That's where we're going," Vänna says. But the boy doesn't seem to notice the tip of the lighthouse and if he does, he doesn't seem to understand.

She sees him fidgeting, moving his shoulders such that his back rubs against his stolen jersey. She reaches over and pulls the back of the jersey's neck, revealing a swath of dead brown skin, the remnants of a sunburn.

She eases the shirt off his back. Flakes cover the entirety of the boy's back and shoulders. Here and there little peels of it curl upward from the reddening skin beneath. Vänna pinches one of the curls. It feels of nothing.

From across his middle back she peels away a patch the size of her palm, thin and fragile as a spiderweb. It comes off easily. She holds it up to the light, and in the light she sees that it is not brown at all, but a translucent thing. She reaches over the boy's shoulder and hands him his skin. He gives her a look of mock disgust, but quickly he takes and inspects it—its microscopic rivulets, its infinite lightness. Then he crumples it up and tosses it on the ground.

They sit awhile like this, Vänna softly pulling away at the skin a previous day's sunlight has killed, relieving the boy's discomfort. Amir sits quietly, skimming through the books Madame El Ward gave him. None hold his interest until he comes across a children's comic book, at the sight of which he lets out a gleeful little cry.

"*Zaytoon wa Zaytoona*," he says, waving the book behind him. Vänna looks at the cover, a drawing of a little boy and girl, their surroundings a place Vänna can't identify, but guesses to be the country of Amir's birth.

She smiles and nods, trying to match the boy's excitement. He repeats the book's title a couple more times, and when Vänna tries to do it, he laughs at her mispronunciation.

Amir points at himself. "Zaytoon," he says. Then he points at her. "Zaytoona."

"All right, Zaytoon, all right," she says.

Amir turns back around and skims the book. Vänna returns to peeling the dead skin from his back. Soon there are only patches of red across his shoulders and back where the heat still lingers. She helps him put the stolen jersey back on.

Outside, to the south, they hear movement. Vänna expected it sooner—the sun is high and bright now, the tourists would be starting to fill the beach, and inevitably some of the more adventurous ones would wander outside the hotel's manicured confines to go exploring.

She leans out. At the edge of the beach she sees a few tourists, some splayed out on lounge chairs and beach towels, others wading into the water. Among them there are soldiers moving, inspecting the area, questioning the hotel's guests and employees. She sees Colonel Kethros.

Before Vänna can turn and grab Amir, the boy is tugging at her arm. He's seen the soldiers too, recognized them by their uniforms as men no different from the ones who chased him through the forest a day earlier.

He stares at Vänna, a terrible urgency about him, and then points northward, away from the uniformed men.

"*Yallah,*" he says.

The children cram their books and their pillowcase of remaining food into their backpack and leave everything else behind. They head north, keeping to the coastline, away from the single road that meanders toward the northeast edge of the island. It is slow going, the rocks pushing outward into the sea in such a way as to force the children to hike up their clothes and step through and over the small tidepools and underwater embankments. But everywhere the sea is clear and they are able to see where their feet make landing.

After a half hour Vänna looks back and, seeing the twisting shoreline behind her, begins to relax. It seems unlikely the colonel and his soldiers saw them.

Soon the rocky outcroppings recede and the children find themselves at another sandy beach, this one open to the public and busy with locals and tourists in the midday heat. Other children, both Amir's age and Vänna's, scurry around, building sandcastles and playing tag. They observe Vänna and Amir with the cautious curiosity that in childhood precedes the making of friendships.

A couple sitting on beach towels nearby smile as Vänna and Amir pass. One of them, a man wearing garish tropical shorts and a T-shirt bearing the name of some other place he once went on vacation, points to Amir's jersey and gives a thumbs-up.

"A Cleveland boy!" he says. "Think they'll win Central next year?"

Amir looks at the man with total confusion. The children keep walking.

A mile or so north of the beach the hillsides become lower and the road traversing them swings close to the shoreline. From here anyone driving can spot the children. Seeing this, Vänna takes Amir's hand. She quickens her pace.

In a clearing they see a deserted cabin set amid a bloom of yellow saltflowers. Vänna leads them to it. Up close it appears to be a fisherman's shack, made of stone and wood and a weathered tin awning. They settle inside and rest their feet, take shelter from the blistering sun.

Vänna retrieves the pillowcase from the backpack and empties it on the floor. For lunch they eat a packet of almonds and another of bitter-chocolate truffles that Vänna strongly suspects are alcoholic. But the boy, who wolfs them down, doesn't seem to mind, and so neither does she.

Through the shack's north-facing window the tip of the island is now clear to see. In a mile or so the land narrows until it is barely wider than the road itself, and this narrowing creates two mushrooms of land, each a near-island in and of itself. At the northeast corner of the second island the ancient lighthouse marks the coast. Tomorrow, at a dock very close to this place, the ferryman will come. All that stands between them and the lighthouse now is a few hours' walking, over the hills and through the ruins.

She watches Amir wandering around the shoreline,

picking the saltflowers. They are a species native to the island; in the summer their flame-shaped petals harden and fall, and it is a favorite pastime of the local children to run through the fields trampling them, the sound of it like firecrackers going off.

She walks outside to join him. He hands her a small bouquet.

Vänna smiles. "Thank you," she says.

They hear a rustling in the brush behind the fisherman's shack. They move to get out of sight, but the only shelter is the shack and to go to it is to go closer to the source of the sound. So they stay in place, watching the leaves rattle and part. They prepare to run.

At first they don't see the thing emerging; it's too slow, too low to the ground, too much the color of the brush. And when finally they do, it's not the eyes or the teeth or the claws they see first, but the scales. A line of bruise-green plates rise from the animal's back. It looks prehistoric, its claws and tail tracing ruts through the sand as it shuffles out into the clearing. Vänna has never seen it before, but it looks as she imagined it would, the bird-eating thing.

It notices them, but it doesn't charge, doesn't gnash its teeth or make any kind of sound. It simply observes them for a moment and then, unhurried, turns and crawls upland. The children watch it as it climbs and disappears behind a well of rocks and into a tidepool, and then over the other end and into a half-submerged cave.

And then they are alone again, hidden from the road by the old fishing shack and the brush. The only sound is of the waves coming and going. They kick off their shoes and sit awhile, enjoying the warmth, skimming stones. And then they set off, northward.

It takes another three hours of hiking until, exhausted, their feet blistered and the daylight all but gone, Vänna and Amir reach the lighthouse. It stands on a high, pedestal-shaped mound that extends past the mainland, and appears to the children as they come up the final rise as a hovering thing.

Vänna motions to the stone structure and Amir, who has for the past hour walked glumly with his head down, brightens a little at the sight of their destination. The children walk to the entrance. Here, at the end of the island, where the hotel and time-share developers have yet to break ground, there are no other people to be seen—not locals, not tourists, nobody—and so complete is this emptiness that it's possible for Vänna to momentarily believe the entire island is theirs alone.

They climb a jagged, crumbling stone staircase that winds around and up the lighthouse, terminating in a vacant lantern room about thirty feet up. By the time they climb inside, the sun has set.

A thick spiked vine grows out of a crack in the stone floor; otherwise the lantern room is empty. Vänna reaches down and grabs the weed between the spikes and pulls it out. She places the backpack down on the ground for Amir to use as a pillow. The boy, drained from the day's walk, lies down and makes no complaint about the unforgiving stone floor. She lies down next to him; she fishes the translation book from their backpack and they try for a while to find a place where their languages meet. She pieces together from various pages the boy's words for *home* and *tomorrow*, and he understands because he finds and mouths her word for *thank you,* and she can sense in him the gratitude, of which she has never been the recipient before and it feels good, feels cleansing. In truth she has no idea where the ferryman will take him, whether he will ever see his family or his home again, but she doesn't for even a minute consider telling this truth because the truth is bereft of kindness while the lie is nothing but.

They tire of words; they turn to pictures. Lazily they flip through the adventures of Zaytoon and Zaytoona, their impossible inventions and miraculous escapes, until Amir can no longer keep his eyes open.

Vänna sits up and looks out at the land to the west. Beyond a small stretch of terrace trees is the place Madame El Ward told her to go. In the morning they will meet the ferryman, and he will know where to take the boy. And only after she's made sure of this will Vänna return to her own home and face the consequences of what she's done. She doesn't much care what those consequences will be, and she enjoys the sensation of not caring, the lightness and sharpness of it.

In the middle of the night she wakes and sees them, the luminous things. Delirious with sleep, she hears a commotion on the beach to the south. She looks out the lantern room's window, where below floats an electric cloud of bright-blue fireflies. They move in erratic flight paths, this way and that, low over the sand and the surf—a dreamlike hovering marked with the sound of hushed conversation. In a moment her eyes adjust, and Vänna sees the fireflies have grown arms beneath them, and those arms have grown bodies.

Slowly the migrants appear out of the night, standing by their beaten rubber dinghy on the otherwise deserted beach. Hands held high, they struggle to find a signal, a means of calling their families back home, confirming they've survived the passage, confirming they've lived.

In time the light of the fireflies begins to disperse. The migrants start walking, headed in the direction of the Hotel Xenios to the south. Vänna watches this movement until it is over and the darkness once more total, then she lies back down and falls asleep. And when the morning comes the afterimage of what she's seen strikes her as so incongruent, so much the fabric of a dream, she quickly comes to believe she never saw it at all.

Chapter Twenty

Before

The human topology of the upper deck shifted as Mohamed enlisted a few men to shuffle over to the port side. He motioned to Walid and Maher.

"Let's go," he said. "Make yourselves useful."

"What are we going to do?" Maher asked.

"You know exactly what we're going to do."

The two men joined a couple others and Mohamed by the old man's side. This time, none of the passengers complained when they stepped around them or pushed against them. They were obliging; they shifted to let the men pass, to let them do this work.

Mohamed nudged the old man with his foot, eliciting no response. He knelt down and slapped the old man a couple of times. He waited a moment, then he stood back up.

"All right," he said, pointing at Maher and Walid first, then the two other men he'd drafted. "You two take the legs, you two take the arms. Kamal and I will hold up the middle."

Umm Ibrahim stood up. "You can't," she said.

"Don't start," Mohamed replied. "Please don't start."

"What are you? Do you not have a God?" Umm Ibrahim shoved her neighboring passenger aside and moved such that she was now as close to the old man as the others who were readying to lift him. She put her hand on his shoulder as though claiming an empty seat. "Just let him sit here until we land. He deserves a proper burial."

"He won't get a proper burial where we're going," Mohamed said. "He'll get a fridge."

Mohamed addressed the men standing around him. "Are you Muslims?" he asked.

Kamal, Walid and a couple of the other men nodded. Maher shrugged.

"Good enough," Mohamed said. He turned back to Umm Ibrahim. "You want him laid to rest by people of his religion or a bunch of Christian strangers?"

Umm Ibrahim said nothing. Mohamed knelt down. With efficient movements he eased the old man's body such that he lay flat on the deck. As the dead body uncurled, the living bodies around it moved away, as though the old man had died of some contagion, some invisible leech still hungry.

"On three, lift," Mohamed ordered. The other men positioned themselves around the corpse, ready to comply.

"Hold on a minute," Walid said.

"What is it?" Mohamed replied.

"Maybe . . ." Walid stammered. "Maybe he has something. We should check."

Mohamed stood up. "Are you serious?"

"Don't look at me like that," Walid said. "Everyone here is thinking it. What, better the fish should keep it?"

Mohamed stepped close to Walid, who stumbled back a few steps. But just as fast Mohamed turned and knelt down by the old man. He checked the solitary pocket on the man's galabeya. Its only contents were an empty box of Tic Tacs and a folded piece of paper. On the paper was written a phone number with a German country code and the name *Basboosa* written atop it.

Mohamed waved these things at Walid. "You want this?" he asked. Walid looked away.

Mohamed threw the empty box of Tic Tacs off the side of the boat and folded the paper again and came to place it back in the old man's pocket, then stopped. He handed it instead to Umm Ibrahim.

"You want to do something for him?" he said. "Here. When you land, make the call. Let them know."

Umm Ibrahim took the paper. Just as Mohamed began readying to lift the old man once more, he heard Walid inhale breath.

"I swear to God . . ." he yelled. "What is it now?"

"The socks," Walid said.

Mohamed stared at Walid. "You tiny, tiny man," he said.

Mohamed knelt down and took the socks the man had been using as gloves. He crumpled them together and threw them at Walid. "Take them and go back to your corner. You say another word for the rest of the trip and I'll throw you overboard myself."

Walid picked up the socks and shuffled back to the

place where he'd been sitting. He looked at no one and no one looked at him.

They lifted the old man, struggling against the weight his slight frame seemed to have taken on since death. They held him as still as they could, balanced lengthwise along the splintered railing, half of him flying.

"Someone say a prayer," Mohamed shouted.

"Which prayer?" Maher replied.

"Any goddamned prayer."

Awkwardly, as he supported one of the old man's legs, Maher recited the opening chapter of the Quran. He had long ago abandoned all but literary interest in his faith, and what he recited now he knew only because it had been drilled into him as a child, and although his memory failed him and he recited the final verses wrong, beseeching the Lord to offer the straight path to both those He blessed and those who angered Him, and although many of the passengers on the boat knew that he had spoken the prayer incorrectly, none said a word except in unison when he was finished. A loud and single-voiced *Ameen* accompanied the old man off the boat and into the water.

Some of the passengers watched, others looked away, pretending nothing had happened at all. A few of them leaned over the edge, and the boat leaned with them. Amir struggled to get between the bodies and press himself against the railing for a look, but Umm Ibrahim held him back. Shielded this way by the lip of the woman's garment, Amir only heard the sound of the body departing. A bloated lash, an interloping wave.

The old man faded into ripples. In the final moments

before the glow of the boat's lantern left him, he seemed to detach from himself, to become two distinct absences: one a trick of memory and light along the surface, the other a vessel of flesh sinking to the floor.

The boat sailed on. The men who'd done the burial returned to their places. For a while it was quiet, until Umm Ibrahim, who had never taken her eyes off Mohamed, spoke.

"I'm glad you'll die along with the rest of us," she said.

Mohamed sat with his eyes closed, his head back against the railing. He did not reply.

"I should have walked to the West," Umm Ibrahim said. "Better to have died on land than out here with the likes of you. I should have walked to the West and when I got there I should have thrown myself at their mercy."

Mohamed laughed. "What mercy, lady? I promise you, they don't give a shit about you or that kid you're carrying inside you."

Amir felt a sharp shove. Before he had lifted himself up he saw Umm Ibrahim moving quickly in Mohamed's direction. Some of the passengers tried to hold her back but could not do so before she reached the smugglers' apprentice and spat in his face.

Mohamed jumped up and grabbed Umm Ibrahim by the throat. He held her like that until the panicked passengers around them pulled him away. Mohamed and two of the men holding him fell back against the pole on which the lantern hung. The lantern fell to the ground and smashed open. Pieces of broken glass littered the rear end of the deck. The passengers leapt back, and the boat shook.

Mohamed shoved the men aside. A trickle of blood ran down his forearm from where the lantern glass had cut him. He stood, teeth bared, one hand on the pistol at his side, the other pointing at Umm Ibrahim, pointing at everyone.

"You sad, stupid people," he said. "Look what you've done to yourselves. The West you talk about doesn't exist. It's a fairy tale, a fantasy you sell yourself because the alternative is to admit that you're the least important character in your own story. You invent an entire world because your conscience demands it, you invent good people and bad people and you draw a neat line between them because your simplistic morality demands it. But the two kinds of people in this world aren't good and bad—they're engines and fuel. Go ahead, change your country, change your name, change your accent, pull the skin right off your bones, but in their eyes they will always be engines and you will always, always be fuel."

Mohamed stopped. He looked around him, saw the way in which all those who had earlier tried to hold him back had now backed away from him. Watching them, he felt some disgust at himself for having lost his composure, for having laid hands on a woman and having yelled this way at the passengers, who were, at the end of the day, customers, people no different than those he would rely on to make a living should he survive this apprenticeship and save enough money to run his own migrant fleet one day. But the men and women who shrank from him now, as though from a rabid, frothing animal, had barely heard a single thing he'd said. They stared only at his hand on the holster, at the gun by his side.

"Anyway, there's nothing to be done," Mohamed said quietly as he slumped back in his place at the stern. "People live, people die. Believe in whatever you want, but for now sit down. The boat is old and won't take much more."

The passengers quieted, the boat sailed, its diesel engine sputtering. Walid picked the flashlight off the floor and hung it up again. With the lantern shattered, its light was now a solitary beam. Only a while later did Maher, looking up from his book of apocryphal scripture, break the silence.

"One should try to believe in things," he said, "even if they let you down afterward."

"What?" Mohamed replied.

"It's something my favorite author once said."

Mohamed closed his eyes. "Your favorite author is wrong," he said.

Under light snow the migrants journeyed. Some leaned against each other and slept, some fixed an endless stare at the horizon, searching for land. But despite the exhaustion and the hunger and the deep and deepening fear, in the smallest way they were a little less cramped. In the smallest way they each now had a little more room.

Chapter Twenty-one

After

Colonel Kethros squats and enters the cave. He picks up the empty cookie wrappers. He touches the lounge-chair cushions with the back of his hand, feeling for residual heat.

"Excuse me, Colonel," says Nicholas, who stands outside, a cell phone in hand. "It's the minister's office, sir."

Kethros lifts the cushions, sweeps his hand across the sand underneath, searching.

"Sir . . ."

Kethros stands. He backs out of the cave and walks over to his soldier. He takes the cell phone from Nicholas's hand; he hangs up.

Nicholas stammers a little. "They say the latest migrant ship has been spotted again," he says. "They want you to reestablish the command center at the beach. . . ."

Kethros shakes his head, silencing the soldier. "What did the housekeeper say?" he asks.

"She says she didn't see anything, sir."

"She was the only one working the night shift yesterday?"

"Yes, sir."

The colonel walks past his subordinate. He stands at the water's edge.

"Do you know what makes them dangerous?" he asks.

"I'm sorry, sir?" Nicholas replies.

"The illegals. Do you know what makes them dangerous?"

Nicholas begins to say something, then stops. Finally he mumbles, "They come here illegally, sir."

The colonel laughs. "Nicholas, you'll make a good officer one day," he says.

He puts his arm around Nicholas's shoulders and hands him a couple of empty wrappers. "Tell Elias and Alexander to show this to the housekeeper, and ask her again. If she still says she didn't see anything, tell them to bring her to me."

Nicholas stares at the wrappers. "Yes, sir," he says.

The colonel pats the soldier on the back, then turns and begins walking up the beach. "When you're done, the four of you get in the truck and drive north. Tell Andreas I'll meet you at Mirror Bay—he'll know where to go."

He walks a few steps, then stops. He waits for the sound of the soldier leaving, and when he doesn't hear it, he turns to find Nicholas still standing there.

"Is there a problem, soldier?"

"It's just . . ." Nicholas pauses.

"Say what's on your mind."

"Why are we doing this?"

Kethros pauses. He looks over the boy's uniform, decorated at the breast with a patch the military hands out to all the soldiers assigned this kind of duty. It features an illustration of an oversize wave, white-capped and curling, its destination a bucolic little village on the shore.

"Nicholas," Kethros says, "you can either ask that question or wear that uniform, but you can't do both."

He leaves the soldiers and walks northward. He traverses the sharp, rocky outcroppings, steadying himself as his false leg struggles to find footing. He knows, although he sees no sign of them, that this is the path the children took. He knows it's only a matter of time.

When he was a child the shoreline was different, he's sure of it. He has a vivid memory of a comma-shaped spit that curled out a hundred feet into the water at low tide, the sand almost white, almost colorless. He remembers playing with the other boys, picking a spot about halfway down and building as big a dam of sand and rocks as they could while watching the tide come in, then seeing how long their construction would withstand the inevitable drowning. He remembers these moments and is certain they took place right here, right in this spot where now there's only a smatter of anemone pools and sharp black rocks.

Soon the outcroppings give way to a public beach and this too he remembers as something different, a staging ground for evacuation drills in preparation for war or fire or natural disaster. He can't recall the specific calamity from which he and his classmates were being trained to escape, only the act of marching in line from the school grounds to this beach, and the sound of giggling and shouting and a high-pitched whistle, a teacher yelling, Let's go, let's go.

Now the place is overrun with tourists and locals. The sand is a loose mosaic of beach towels and coolers and shoes with money and keys stuffed in the toes. He has always been able to tell them apart, the tourists and the locals, but now it is by their appearance, the wealth implied in the tourists' clothing and their accessories and their pristine rented cars, whereas before it was by something in the marrow of them. It induces a kind of nausea in the colonel to see it, to see how nondescript these foreigners and their money and their utter absence of culture have made his island, his people.

"Is something wrong?"

The colonel starts. A middle-aged woman he recognizes from town eyes him.

"I'm sorry?" he says.

"It's just . . ." She points at his uniform. "I thought something might be wrong. More, you know, problems like yesterday."

Kethros smiles, regains his composure. "Nothing's wrong at all," he says. "Beautiful day, isn't it?"

The woman smiles back, laughs in relief. "I was worried there might be more," she says, leaning in as though to tell a secret. "It feels like it's every day now."

The colonel rubs the woman's shoulder. "Enjoy the weather," he says. "We won't get much more of this before summer rolls in."

He walks up to the beachside road and buys a drink

from one of the vendors. He sits on the hollow trunk of a dead sleep-gum tree and he passes an hour watching the beachgoers. His phone rings incessantly but he ignores it. A couple of locals who recognize him wave in his direction but he ignores them too. He ignores the sounds of the sunheads, a scramble pattern of black wings above, their high, brittle discontent; he ignores the hustler who walks the beach with a cigarette-girl tray hanging over his chest, selling watered-down sunscreen and sunflower seeds in violation of local ordinance. He simply stares out at the sea, lets it blur and double in his vision until it swallows the land and the sky, until there's nothing else. This arpeggio spring, April staircasing away. It used to feel smoother, the ending of winter, the island in rebirth.

A young girl bobs in the surf, about fifty feet from shore. She looks calm but she is drowning. The colonel has seen it before, the way people appear so in control just before they go under. No one else seems to notice, not even the swimmers near her. She rises once, dips below the surface, rises once more and is gone.

The colonel stands up. He tosses his drink and sprints to the water. He shoves a couple of tourists out of his way, tramples over a spread of finger sandwiches and cookies laid on a checkered tablecloth. People yell, but no one tries to stop him. They can see where he's headed, they start to extrapolate.

The colonel runs into the surf. He dives, slicing through an oncoming wave. He has been a swimmer since before he could walk, and although he has done it only a few times since he lost his leg, alone at night in the less-frequented lagoons of the island, that feeling of being at home in the water, of being *fluent,* never goes away. He moves effortlessly, stroke over stroke, until he reaches the girl's limp body. He wraps his arm around her chest; he pulls her back.

At the shore the beachgoers have gathered to watch as the colonel, his uniform drenched, carries the girl out of the water. There are gasps from the crowd when they see her, the smallness of her, and someone says, Call an ambulance, but no one moves. No one can let go of the watching.

The colonel lays the girl down on the sand. She shows no sign of breathing. Remnants of the colonel's cadet training come to him; he eases the girl's head back, lets her jaw relax. He finds the tip of her breastbone, laces his fingers together and presses down with the weight of both arms on one palm. He begins to push, keeping to the rhythm he was taught, somewhere between once and twice a second. There is something exhausting about it, not only the physical act itself but this being on the other side of a life, being so close to departure.

After thirty compressions he stops. He pries the girl's mouth open, breathes twice into her airway, then goes back to compressions. He's heard the training has changed in recent years, that now you're supposed to do nothing but chest compressions, or perhaps it is nothing but breathing. It doesn't matter—he does what he was taught. The girl doesn't move.

In his periphery he sees one of the tourists flag down a passing military jeep. The soldiers who get out of the vehicle are his. At first they don't see him behind the assembled crowd, but when they do, they come running down to the shoreline.

"Let's get her in the truck," Elias says, kneeling by the colonel's side. He digs his hand into the sand beneath the girl and begins to lift her up, until Kethros shoves him violently away. The soldier falls over; he backs off, becomes one of the watchers.

The colonel continues compressing the girl's chest. She doesn't move. He keeps going, aware now of a wailing from nearby—the girl's mother, who between sobs is screaming, "Do something, do something," at no one at all.

The colonel keeps pressing. There is among the crowd now a sense of time's unbearable weight, of too much having passed. At the rear of the assemblage a few people start to walk away.

Then a sputtering fountain of salt water comes out of the girl's mouth, and on its heels, breath. She wakes in spasms, coughing and reaching for air. Immediately the colonel turns her onto her side. As spittle leaks out of her mouth, he bends down and whispers in her ear: "Easy, easy. Just breathe."

The girl's mother drops to her knees and wraps her arms around her daughter, so tightly that Kethros is forced to pull them apart so as to give the girl some room for air. The girl's father too takes a knee, though in his restraint he comes off awkward and self-conscious, more embarrassed than relieved. Quickly he stands up and tries to shake the colonel's hand.

"I don't know how we can ever . . ." he starts, but Kethros cuts him off.

"Are you from here?" the colonel asks.

"I'm sorry?"

Kethros points at the island's interior. "Are you *from here*?"

"Born and raised," the man says. "Ten generations."

In one swift motion the colonel slaps the man across the face, again and again, until his four soldiers intervene. Released from Kethros's grip, the man appears stunned and humiliated and utterly uncomprehending.

"Then act from here," the colonel says as his soldiers pull him away.

They drive back to the temporary encampment at Revel beach, where Colonel Kethros showers in one of the outdoor stalls and changes into a clean uniform. When he returns to the command center his soldiers are waiting.

"Go home," he says. "Come back tomorrow at sunrise. We'll head up north and find the boy then."

The soldiers disperse without a word.

In the makeshift camp the police officers and city morgue workers are clearing out the caution tape and folding up the unused body bags. A printer, out of paper, beeps ceaselessly; the colonel unplugs it. He checks the messages on his phone, and deletes them all. He walks over to the Hotel Xenios restaurant and orders a rib eye and drinks a couple of beers and then goes to the beach where a day earlier the bodies washed up. The hotel has put the lounge chairs back, along with a sign apologizing for the inconvenience. He lies on one of the lounge chairs.

It is pitch black when he startles awake at the sound of footsteps. He turns to find Nicholas.

"What time is it?" the colonel asks.

"Three-thirty," Nicholas replies.

"What are you doing here?"

Nicholas points northward. "Another raft has landed," he says.

Chapter Twenty-two

Before

Amir shivered. What had started as a light snowfall now turned to dousing sleet that seemed to come from all directions; his clothes and his life jacket became soaked once more. He put his arms around his knees and became as small as he could muster. The dark, near-total, lulled his eyes into following the jagged run of the hanging flashlight, and this, coupled with the wild rocking of the boat and the chaotic shouts of its passengers, quickly brought about nausea. He burst into a heaving cough but there was nothing in him to vomit.

Even in the chaos that overwhelmed the upper deck, he could hear the sounds of the people trapped below. Earlier, when the snow first fell and the sea started turning violent, their shouting had come through the boards muffled and distant. But it was clearer now, so much so that Amir could differentiate between the voices, and in doing so imagined those beneath him not as a single impossible organism but as individual people, bound by their confines but solitary in their fear.

It occurred to Amir then why he could suddenly hear the lower-deck captives with such clarity—something else had gone quiet. Gone was the ceaseless wheezing, so constant over the past two days that the upper-deck passengers had all but become desensitized to it. Gone was the stink of diesel. The engine had stopped running. Amir looked around to see if anyone else had noticed, but everyone he saw in the momentary illumination of the wandering flashlight appeared to be otherwise concerned. Even Teddy, who must have known, was busy wrestling the wheel, desperately trying to keep the compass pointed in the direction of *N*.

So violently did the snow turn to storm that at first nobody noticed Kamal had managed to make a call. In desperation, using a phone he'd believed had run out of minutes, he tried the emergency number again.

The boat heaved and deflated, each passenger bracing against the other and against the boat's own battered sides. With no glass lantern left to refract its beam, the flashlight, which had previously brought some respite from the darkness, now swung wildly from where it hung, the light landing on each passenger at random, solitary and intense as an interrogator's lamp.

"Keep calm," Mohamed shouted, wrapping his forearm around a run of knotted rope. "Do you want to die out here? Keep calm!"

But he had lost them now, had lost their superficial obedience. Even the gun that dug its barrel into his thigh every time a wave slapped the hull forfeited its malicious authority. Because now the men and women, who, in undertaking this passage, had shed their belongings and their roots and their safety and their place of purpose and all claim to agency over their own being, had now finally shed their future. There was nothing left for the smugglers' apprentice to threaten, nothing he could leverage.

Instead it was Kamal who managed to produce something of a pause in the commotion. "Shut up, shut up," he said. "I have them on the phone."

The passengers in Kamal's immediate vicinity turned to look at the bare blue glow emanating from the screen. They observed it the way a doll maker might observe a creation come to life.

"Hello, yes, hello," Kamal yelled in English over the sound of the waves and the wind. "My name Kamal. We call from boat. You make help, you make help."

From where he sat, pressed hard against the railing, Walid swiped for the phone. "Give me that, you idiot," he said. "You don't know what you're doing."

Kamal pushed Walid away. He motioned for silence. He listened.

"Speak to them in Arabic," Walid said. "They have people who speak Arabic."

Kamal ignored him. He pressed the phone against his one ear and cupped his hand over the other, struggling to make out the voice on the line. His face contorted into a confused frown.

"Boat," he said feebly. "Boat for West."

Maher reached over and motioned for the phone. Kamal looked at him, reluctant.

"You've heard me speak English," Maher said. Kamal

handed him the phone. Like a glowing totem it dragged the eyes of the passengers along with it. All of them, even Mohamed, watched in silence as Maher spoke.

"We are stranded somewhere south of the continent," Maher said. He leaned on that distorted Oxford English accent that bound so much of the previously colonized world, from North Africa to India to all the places over which the sun never set, in each place tinted with turns of the local tongue but still possessed of its most potent quality, a veneer of implied civility, that gentlemanly air. "Our destination was the island of Kos but we don't know where we are. We have a child and a pregnant woman onboard and we need help."

Only a few of the passengers understood what Maher said, but those who didn't took comfort in the quantity and velocity of the spoken words, as though no Westerner could possibly refuse assistance to anyone who spoke the language so well.

Maher listened and nodded in response to some incoming query. He looked around the boat, his lips moving silently.

"About a hundred, maybe more," he said.

Again he listened, and again came another query. Maher studied the faces of the people around him.

"Everywhere," he said.

A massive wave lifted the *Calypso* high. In its wake the violence of the drop rattled the phone loose from Maher's hand. It skittered along the deck and into the hands of a nearby passenger, who upon righting himself handed it back to Maher quickly and with a kind of fearful gentleness, as though he were holding a newborn or a piece of radioactive ore.

Maher put the phone back to his ear. He listened a long time. He gave the phone back to Kamal.

"They're gone," he said.

Kamal grabbed the phone and began trying to redial the number, but after a few rings the device gave a vibrating shrug and the screen went black, the battery depleted.

For a moment the passengers kept their eye on the phone, even as Kamal tossed it on the deck, as if the collective gaze, powered by enough desperation, could prove resuscitative.

"It doesn't matter, they wouldn't have . . ." Walid began, then stopped. He stared at his hands, gloved in a stranger's socks.

No one bothered to ask who it was Kamal had dialed. Some assumed it was a national coast guard, or perhaps whatever arm of the United Nations was supposed to deal with such things. Or maybe it was a private charity, something like Doctors Without Borders or the Christian groups that took on the names of saints and angels. Or maybe Kamal had simply called a random number. It didn't much matter; the voice on the other end of the line, which to all but two of the passengers went unheard, was all of these things. It was the world.

"Wait a minute, wait a minute," Umm Ibrahim said. "This means we're close, right? If we weren't close to land, we wouldn't have reached them in the first place."

Some of the passengers stopped to consider this, but in the absence of any signs of life on the horizon, it was of little comfort.

Amir leaned his head against the boards. He listened to the shouting and pleading below. He thought of Quiet Uncle, blind among blind bodies, caught in this punishment of a journey—the sea endlessly receding below, the fruit of the upper deck endlessly out of reach.

He reached his fingers through the boards. The hand of his uncle met them.

"It's going to be all right," Quiet Uncle said.

"Stop saying that," Amir replied. "I want to go home. I want to go home."

Amir cried. There was nothing to it, a whimpering lost in the storm.

"Listen to me," Quiet Uncle said. "Listen—I know the nickname you gave me. I know what you called me when I wasn't around. And you're right. I thought I could hide my way through life, I thought my brothers were selfish and stupid for speaking up. But the truth is we're all selfish and stupid."

A wave washed over the railing. The water fell through the cracks into the lower decks. Amir coughed the salt water out of his mouth.

"Pay attention—there isn't time," Quiet Uncle said. "Whatever happens, you have to promise me you'll do whatever you have to do. Whatever kind of person you need to be—quiet, loud, violent, invisible—you be that person. Promise me."

Another wave crashed. Amir tried to lift himself up but Quiet Uncle wouldn't let go of his hand.

"Promise me," he said.

"I promise," Amir replied.

The grip on his hand released.

Chapter Twenty-three

After

The workers circle the rubber dinghy, stabbing it at regular intervals. The raft whistles and contracts. When it appears to have no more air left to exhale, the workers begin to roll it up so as to fit it on the waiting flatbed truck. But try as they might, they can't get the craft to compress beyond a certain smallness. Even though they've pulled all the air from inside it, beneath the skin the craft has bones, and the bones won't bend.

"This is it then, the panicking time," one of the workers says to another. "One a month, maybe. One a week, maybe. But three in two days, no. Now they'll start shutting things down, now they'll bring in the real army."

Colonel Kethros stands at the shore. The tide is rising and every other wave licks at the soles of his boots. Like many beaches on the northern end of the island, this one has an isolated, lunar quality about it, visible in the way the rocky, unvegetated hills pen the curving beach, the way not much can be seen from here but the sharply rising land. Considering this, it occurs to the colonel that the migrants who arrived the previous night and immediately set southward in the direction of the Hotel Xenios would not have been able to see the resort when they made landfall here. Instead, they would have likely noticed its lights when they were still farther out to sea, their raft still drifting. And once they made landfall, they would have simply walked toward where the lights should be, even though they could no longer see them. They would have navigated not by sight but by faith.

Elias and Alexander stand at the side of the road by the truck, doing nothing. Like Andreas, they have spent plenty of time on this part of the island but have so far proven useless, unable to provide the colonel with even the most basic information when he asked where in these parts children were likely to congregate. One of the twins suggested the edge of the eastern inlet, where tourists sometimes went so their kids could jump off the small protruding rocks into the turquoise water, but the colonel dismissed this—the inlet was too public, too close to the main road. No, the colonel said, where in this place are children likely to congregate *in secret*? But the twins simply looked at each other and shrugged.

Kethros turns his attention to Nicholas, who has decided to make himself useful by helping clear the residue of the migrant landing. Carefully he picks up and folds every piece of discarded, waterlogged clothing before handing it to the workers, who then simply chuck it in the nearest garbage bag. They seem to regard the young soldier as, at best, harmless, and for the most part they ignore him.

The colonel waves at Nicholas, who stops what he's doing.

"Go back and stand with Elias and Alexander by the truck," the colonel says. Nicholas complies.

The colonel's phone rings. He ignores it. Since before sunrise it has been ringing—calls from the capital, from Lina Eliades and from various reporters. What these people expect from him—which of their own uncertainties and anxieties they think he might alleviate—he can't begin to imagine.

The other military truck pulls up to the roadside. Andreas, who the colonel dispatched to fetch coffee, has returned. He parks the truck and walks down the beach to where Kethros stands.

"It's a mess at the Xenios, Colonel," Andreas says. "There's nowhere to put them—even the facility at the old school is full. They've got them sleeping on the sand."

Kethros doesn't reply.

"The ministry called again," Andreas continues. "They want us back at the staging area."

The colonel walks past Andreas and yells at the workers to hurry up. They look feeble and foolish, wrestling with an empty rubber raft, trying to tame a slack, inanimate thing. Watching them engaged this way, the colonel feels the victim of an ongoing chronological prank, a punishment befitting the old myths. It's not the first time he's felt this way. For a week after the amputation of his leg, he suffered from endless hiccups. None of the doctors could explain why, but every few seconds that light seizing came, and by the second day the medical staff needed to sedate him just to keep him from tearing out his tubes and monitors. The surgeon said the body just does these things sometimes, responds this way to the loss of itself.

Now he feels something similar, another punishment without end, whereby he is destined to spend eternity a step behind the happening of things, unable to preempt or even witness any event of import, only bob about help-lessly in its wake.

A black rectangle, half-buried in the sand, catches the colonel's attention. He walks over and picks it up—a cell phone, the old kind, with fat physical buttons on its front, the kind most Westerners left behind a decade earlier. It's clear the sand and salt water have rendered the thing unusable, the screen scratched away to nothing, most of the buttons missing.

He turns the phone over in his hand. Written on the back in permanent marker is a phone number he recog-nizes immediately. It's the emergency desk at the coast guard office.

For most of the last year, this was how it has worked—once the migrants sensed they were nearing land, they would call this number, say they were in distress, and wait for the ships to come out and get them, the phone's signal a kind of invisible flare. That the coast guard often couldn't pinpoint the signal with any accuracy, that often the signal itself disappeared well before they could get to its location—none of this mattered much. At some point the strategy worked its way into the pas-sage's unwritten guidebook. Such knowledge seemed to spread through osmosis, a communal knowing. Only in recent months has the practice abated somewhat, in part because the number of vigilante boats prowling the coast has increased, and it is becoming more and more difficult for the migrants awaiting rescue to tell good ships from bad.

The colonel tosses the phone into one of the garbage bags by the side of the truck.

"That's good enough," he says to the workers, who have managed to awkwardly bundle up half the raft with duct tape. "Get it on the truck and let's go."

The workers comply. Soon the truck is backing onto the road and heading south toward the main island. The colonel and his soldiers get in their vehicles and follow.

Riding in the front jeep with Andreas driving, the colonel observes the bare northeast corner of the island receding in the side mirror.

Recently he's come down with phantom pains. At unpredictable intervals a dull sensation seems to crawl up from the empty space within his prosthesis. The last time he felt such a sensation was in the aftermath of the day he awoke in a field hospital corseted in white dressing and emptied of all recent memory. It lasted a long time, the years he spent in slow rehabilitation of both body and mind, relearning the mechanics of balance and unlearning the stubborn, seething rage he felt at both the people who'd sent him to the killing fields and the people he'd failed to defend. How he hated the people he'd failed to defend.

Now the phantom pains return and the colonel attributes their return not to any particular incident, but rather to the general indignities of middle age. On the other side of fifty, he experiences aging as a return, of sorts. With increasing regularity, the past pummels him—memories long dormant resurface for no particular reason and linger for days, and the dull throbbing in his knee he believes to be a physical manifestation of this same phenomenon. He's read somewhere that the makeup of the human body is such that wounds never truly disappear, and that certain diseases of malnourishment, when extreme enough, will cause the skin to spit old scars back up to the surface, the body a secret archive of harm. He wonders now if aging isn't itself a kind of gradual malnourishment, a closing in of things, the past forced violently back to the surface.

The plain weakness of it disgusts him—the way it makes him no better than any other small, ordinary man going through any other small, ordinary midlife crisis—but in truth he knows what he misses most is being young, the nothing days spent fishing in the south-shore lagoons, the nights spent drunk and happy by torch- or firelight in the small, hidden places where the youth of the island have always gone to be alone and alive—the inland ruins or the abandoned mountainside monastery or the lighthouse he sees now receding in the jeep's rear-view mirror.

"Stop the car," the colonel says.

Andreas pulls over to the side of the road. The workers' truck ahead of them continues onward but the soldiers in the jeep behind them stop.

"Turn around," the colonel says. "Go, now. Quickly."

Andreas turns and heads in the opposite direction.

For a moment the vehicles pass each other, and the driver of one shrugs at the driver of the other. Soon both are speeding north.

The colonel points to the lighthouse. "There," he says. "Move, move."

Andreas floors the pedal, his uncertainty about the nature of their purpose giving way to a youthful excitement at the prospect of going fast. In a couple of minutes the trucks pull up to the foot of the stone lighthouse, dust clouds chasing behind them. Before the truck stops, the colonel is out and moving. In his half-pivoting gait he hurries not toward the lighthouse but to the edge of the nearby forest, where he sees the fleeting glimmer of two shades of gold—blond strands of hair and a shimmering necklace, the boy and girl, running away.

Chapter Twenty-four

Before

The lights appeared first as fog. Only after a while did the individual bulbs become distinguishable, and a small, twinkling line of blue and green and red and orange revealed themselves, suspended just above the waterline. Among those in Amir's corner of the *Calypso,* Umm Ibrahim was the first to see it.

"Look, look," she screamed.

Some of the passengers followed her pointing finger and saw the lights, which for the first time since the massive freight ship passed them the previous night gave a sense of perspective in the otherwise empty sea. The colored bulbs did not stand still; they moved atop the water, rising and falling with the movement of the sea.

"What is it?" said Kamal. He turned to Mohamed. "Are we here? Is this land?"

Mohamed didn't answer. He squinted in the direction of the colored lights. Suddenly, he and a few around him became aware of something else coming from the same source. A repetitive melody, four beats on a tabla followed by the flirty chime of a flute.

"Listen, it's our music," Umm Ibrahim said. "It's 'Khosara, Khosara.' I know it—it's an Egyptian song. It's our people."

"Hold on, hold on," Mohamed said. "We don't know anything yet."

"What's there to know?" Walid replied. He pointed at Teddy, manning the wheel. "Go in their direction," he demanded.

"I can't go in any direction," Teddy said. "The engine is dead."

Walid sat stunned, the tips of the waves crashing over the railing and onto his already-soaked frame.

"Do you have flares?" he asked Mohamed. "A megaphone, some way to reach them?"

"We don't know who they are, you idiot," Mohamed replied. "Everyone knows the Westerners run trap boats. How do you know they're not trying to lure you to them with lights and Arabic music and then sink us all?"

"We're already sinking," Walid yelled. "Look around you—this boat is coming apart. We'll drown out here. Use your gun, fire a few shots in the air—maybe they'll hear us."

"Be quiet," Mohamed replied. He observed the men and women around him, some of whom had started eyeing his weapon. He pressed himself back against the boards. "Don't even think about it," he said.

A huge wave crashed onto the deck. Water rushed down through the cracks.

Another set of lights began to materialize on the horizon. A strip of blue and white neon, perhaps a couple hundred feet behind the suspended colored bulbs and a little higher up, as though perched on a hill. Between them the two sources of illumination gave evidence of land that could not yet be seen. Whereas the colored bulbs bobbed and bounced, the blue and white neon remained in place. Soon some of the passengers began to understand what it was they were looking at—a boat, docked on the shore, and behind it a structure, the beginnings of land, only a mile or two away.

"Get back from the edge," Mohamed screamed. "Get back from . . ." But there was no one listening to him now. Mesmerized by the distant lights, the passengers rushed portside. The boat leaned hard. From among the mass of bodies one man, a young Tunisian, stepped onto the railing and became the first to jump into the sea.

Chapter Twenty-five

After

Amir watches from the lighthouse. The beach, a mile to the south and well downland, looks this morning similar to the one he awoke on two days earlier—here too there are men in uniform standing by the roadside, a hastily constructed cordon to keep gawkers at bay. And even though the workers who scour the beach now are not dressed in the white astronaut suits he remembers seeing, their hands are gloved and their mouths and noses covered. But Amir sees no bodies, no field of human debris, only a few sandals, plastic bags, soiled clothing and a now-mutilated raft. Mechanically, efficiently, the workers collect these things, drop them in large blue garbage bags, and throw the bags onto the waiting truck.

Amir runs his finger along the bell-shaped locket around his neck. In the ceaseless urgency of his time on this island he has succeeded in avoiding the thought of his mother, of where she might be now, of what she must have thought on waking in that still-too-alien seaside city to find half her family gone. But in this moment there is no turning away, and finally facing the absence of his mother, Amir recalls every time he wished ill on her for hitching their future to a man who was family yet not, for abandoning their home, for giving him a brother who was no brother at all. He recalls these times and in doing so feels certain that this is his fault, that he would never have ended up in this place if only he had been better. The island spread out before him, its eastern spine ragged and desolate and wind-lashed, appears now not as a place or even a dream but a punishment. Amir traces the locket around his neck and makes peace with the certainty that if he never leaves this place, never sees his mother again, it will have been his fault.

But the girl says he will leave this place. She says *home,* and he believes her.

He watches as the workers roll and fold the dinghy as much as they are able and then hold it in place with duct tape and lift it onto the truck. In a little while the beach is pristine again, but for a few smears and indentations in the sand—markers of the people who arrived here the night before, fading now in the rising tide.

The truck departs. As it backs onto the road, it emits a loud beeping noise and the noise startles Vänna awake. Slowly she shakes the sleep off. Unable to tell how late in the morning it is and worried they might miss the ferry-man, she quickly gathers her things into the backpack. She steps out onto the walkway that circles the lantern room, where Amir is standing by the railing, watching a truck and a pair of military jeeps driving away.

And then, suddenly, the jeeps stop. They turn back and race in the direction of the lighthouse.

The children watch, but only for the instant it takes to realize that in this barren quadrant there is no other landmark; the vehicles are headed directly for them.

Vänna grabs Amir by the shoulder. As the two of them turn to run, the backpack slips off Vänna's shoulder over the railing. Its contents spill as it falls, books and magazines spreading their pages winglike, floating down to the sand.

The children run down the staircase and out the lighthouse door. Outside, violent against the cliffsides to the north, the waves crash. The clouds dim the daylight and the canopy of nearby Terrace trees fragment it. They grow nowhere else on the island, these upturned things, the spiked branches perfectly horizontal, longest near the bottom of the trunk, shortest at the top. Morning light, by the time it reaches the floor of the forest, resembles the golden fading that precedes the end of the day. Vänna and Amir sprint westward, toward the forest.

Hand in hand they run blind, the sound of the soldiers closing in behind them. The men, by their movement, radiate something animalistic, a violence of breathing and footfalls. Vänna hears someone give an order to split up, and though the voice has lost all the cool detachment she's come to associate with Colonel Dimitri Kethros, she knows it's him.

Her toe catches against a protruding rock. Pain shoots up her entire left side and she lets out a scream but neither she nor Amir pause. Even as her left sandal dislodges and she feels every inch of ground beneath her, every pebble and twig, she runs.

Behind them the soldiers head along three different

directions, and soon their sounds thin out, so much so that Vänna begins to hope they might have lost the scent. But one persistent echo of footfalls remains on their trail, a single body, he blind to them and they blind to him in the thick of these scaly, leaning trees, but close and closing.

At the very western edge of the forest Vänna and Amir come upon a clutch of high brush. It marks a border of sorts—here the Terrace trees end and the land lowers into a narrow footpath along the northern coast. Vänna can see, just a mile or so along the path, a small boathouse and its weathered dock. Their destination.

She takes Amir by the arm. They step into the brush, the sharp nettles picking and scraping against their skin. They both kneel down, sinking into the brown-green shrubs, becoming inanimate. Amir curls up with his hands around his knees, the way he spent most of his time on the boat journey. Vänna crouches beside him.

They wait. The footfalls that they heard earlier sprinting now slow to a cautious, molasses pace. But the sound grows closer, the soldier inches closer.

Not like this, Vänna thinks, not here. She considers making a break for it, sending Amir in the direction of the boathouse as she lunges at the soldier, tackling him. But there's no use, no hope—she would not keep the soldiers from doing what they've come here to do. They would catch both her and the boy, and what stings more than this certainty or the opposing uncertainty of what they would end up doing to the boy is the simple fact that she has come this far, come this close, and failed.

The footsteps grow closer, then stop. A pair of hands

reach down and spread a gap in the brush. The children and the soldier stare at each other in silence.

Vänna stands. She pulls Amir up. The two children are only a few inches away from the young soldier who's caught them. Vänna recognizes him by his lanky frame—she saw him around the Hotel Xenios a few days earlier and then among the gaggle of Colonel Kethros's subordinates who came to her home. She suspects he is at most five or six years older than she is. He looks a way she doesn't associate with soldiers—not so much weak or fearful or winded from chasing the children through the forest. He looks in pain.

Vänna shifts to her left, such that she stands directly between the soldier and Amir. From elsewhere in the forest come the disjointed voices of the other men yelling, trying to track one another down. Soon they will arrive here, and there is no getting around the fact that they will take the boy but at least she will make sure they can't take him quietly. She's going to make it ugly, she's going to give them a fight.

But the young soldier who stands in front of them makes no reply to the calls coming from the other side of the forest. He simply stares at Amir, then Vänna, then past both children to the little-used footpath that leads to the boathouse.

"Go," he whispers.

Vänna doesn't move. In a span that lasts no more than a second or two but feels eternally longer, she tries to determine whether this is some sort of trick. Or perhaps the soldier is only speaking to her, for whom punishment is temporary and optional, and not the boy, for whom it is neither.

But he speaks again, his voice still a whisper but more urgent now.

"Go."

Vänna grabs Amir. The children back away a few steps from the soldier and then turn and run down the sloping footpath. Nicholas watches them fade from view and fade from earshot, the sound of them swallowed by the sound of the waves. Then he turns around and joins the others.

A dampness spreads out from the place where the flesh of Colonel Kethros's leg meets his prosthesis, and with it a sharp pain. He waits in the disorienting middle of the forest. One by one, his four soldiers return to him, each empty-handed.

A girl's sandal is dislodged on a rock nearby. In this place, so far removed from the beaten path that even the most adventurous tourists have not had the chance to trash it, the sight of such a thing is peculiar, jarring. But in the past year the colonel has seen many similar sights—discarded jackets, shoes worn straight through, underwear soiled from endless days at sea. At almost every migrant ship landing, this phenomenon, this shedding, has become commonplace.

But this is different. This is no foreigner, no illegal. This is the discarded belonging of a local girl, and the colonel feels upon seeing it that the girl has been in some way defiled, that decency itself has been defiled, and that he has let it happen.

Kethros inspects his soldiers, all still struggling to catch their breath even though they've been running only a short while.

"Where did they go?" he asks.

"We didn't see anything," Elias says. His brother nods.

"Nothing," Andreas says.

"Nothing," Nicholas says.

The colonel observes Nicholas, and is again fascinated by the boy. From the moment he arrived in Kethros's unit, the colonel knew Nicholas was not fit to be a soldier. You can see it in his eyes, the way they dart around like the eyes of a stalked deer. It has become frowned upon to call such a thing weakness, but anyway *weakness* is not the right word for what the colonel now sees clearly in the marrow of his young subordinate. It's something else, an absence of something vital.

His father once told him that every man is nothing more or less than the demands he makes of the world, and that the more a man demands of the world, the bigger the magnitude of his success or failure in life. This, his father said, is what matters—the size of the asking. And this is what the colonel thinks of as he studies Nicholas's darting eyes, studies the weight of the lie on him; this is what the word *weakness* can never properly describe— the absolute poverty of the boy's asking, the willingness with which he seems ready to shuffle meekly through the world, making not a single demand. Weakness Kethros can tolerate—this other thing, he can't.

"Where did they go, Nicholas?" he asks.

Nicholas pauses a moment, but there's no fight in him. In shame he points to the western edge of the forest. The colonel sidesteps him and walks through the thicket, until he sees the footpath that leads down to the boathouse.

"Elias, is there a proper road farther inland, one that leads down there?" he asks.

Elias nods.

"Good. You and Alexander come with me. Andreas, take Nicholas back to the staging area. Watch him until I get back."

Andreas approaches Nicholas awkwardly, certain of what the colonel means but uncertain as to how he should behave toward a soldier who until moments ago was one of his own. But before Andreas can say or do anything, the colonel grabs Nicholas, his hand cupping the boy's jaw with such violence, his teeth pressed inward, his lips compressed, and it appears for a moment to the other three soldiers that their commander is trying to crush the lower part of Nicholas's face, to rip it clean from the rest.

But as quickly as it comes, it passes—Kethros releases his grip. He pats Nicholas on the cheek. He smiles, and in a single, purposeful movement he reaches out and rips the patch stitched into the chest of his uniform.

"It's all right, son, it's all right," the colonel says. "Just imagine how little would get done if all men had spines."

Chapter Twenty-six

Before

Amir held on to a rusted cleat on the deck, struggling to keep from sliding portside as wave after wave smashed into the hull behind him. Dexterous claws leapt upward, over the gunwale and down onto the deck, the water digging into the rot-green flesh of the *Calypso*. With every wave the boat tipped farther onto its side, the passengers skittering sideways, the critical angle closing in, after which the vessel would continue its rotation, capsizing.

A deep cracking sound emerged from somewhere below, the hull giving way. As the *Calypso* tilted, the flashlight came loose from its hook and was washed overboard. Only the faint backlit clouds and the distant colored lights of shore provided illumination. The passengers screamed and shouted for help, their voices no sooner escaping the boat than they were swallowed by the storm. To anyone standing at the shore the *Calypso* would have been just another parcel of nighttime, unheard and unseen.

Another man pushed his way through the crowd and

onto the portside railing. He zipped up his orange life vest as high as it would go and then, stumbling as though punch-drunk, he tried to step onto the railing, preparing to dive in pursuit of the Tunisian who moments earlier had made a break for the shore. He managed one foot up before the boat shuddered violently and tilted, throwing him overboard. He tumbled, colliding neck-first with the water, and whether it was the sea or the night that took him, in an instant he vanished from view.

"Stay on the boat, damn you, stay on the boat," Mohamed shouted. "Whoever jumps dies." But as the waves increased in ferocity, washing the deck entirely and shattering the remaining wheelhouse windows, more and more passengers leapt overboard. The ones who'd bought life vests from the smugglers went first, struggling for traction on the sea-slick deck, orienting themselves in the direction of the music and the colored lights. Each after the other in rag-doll posture, they took flight, each after the other they disappeared, the floating world rising up to meet them.

Among those readying to jump, Amir saw Umm Ibrahim. In the bedlam she'd moved portside, the keeling side that dipped with every wave until it neared touching the water. Amir watched her as she steadied herself against a fellow passenger, and then in one motion reached down and pulled her niqab completely off.

Underneath she wore a bright, sleeveless summer dress, decorated with watercolor lilacs. An orange life jacket rested too high on her frame, pushed upward by the rise of her belly. As she stood at the edge, she turned and scanned the deck. The boat righted itself with a falling thud between waves, and the water drained away. There came over the *Calypso* a kind of diastolic silence, a temporary pause. And in this pause Amir and Umm Ibrahim caught eyes.

"Come back," Amir yelled. "Don't go, don't go."

Umm Ibrahim looked at the boy as though she'd never seen him before. She turned and, the boat rising and tilting in her direction, jumped.

As the *Calypso* smashed back onto its hull, a square piece of the deck by the wheelhouse exploded upward. The combination lock that had kept it in place broke open, and suddenly a monster of grasping limbs burst out from the belly of the boat. The passengers confined to the lower decks struggled to escape.

The last screw holding the cleat to which Amir clung came loose. Before he could latch on to any other part of the railing, he was sliding toward portside, toward the water. Screaming, he grabbed at whatever bodies he could, but each shook him off.

Then a pair of arms were around him, arresting his motion. With the weight of both the stranger's body and the righting boat, Amir was slammed down onto the deck, the wind knocked out of him, the boards cracking beneath.

Amir wiped the salt water from his eyes. He saw, looming over him, Walid.

"Give it to me," Walid said.

"What?" Amir replied.

"Give it to me," Walid repeated. "It's useless on you."

With one hand Walid pinned Amir by the throat, with

the other he struggled to loosen the zipper of the boy's life jacket.

"No," Amir screamed. He turned his head and bit down as hard as he could on Walid's finger. He tasted blood.

Walid let out a cry and slapped Amir across the face. He grabbed each side of the boy's life jacket, and with a sharp burst of force, pulled the jacket open. The cheap plastic zipper exploded like confetti; the jacket came undone.

Walid shoved Amir to the side, half turning the boy to slip the jacket from around his arms. In possession of what he was after, he stumbled upward. He put the life jacket on and backed away toward portside, searching out the distant shore, the lights and the music.

Chapter Twenty-seven

After

The footpath, almost never used, is overrun in places with weeds, and sometimes it disappears into a labyrinth of jagged rocks and in one place is made a long, shallow puddle by the encroaching tide. Vänna can feel a cut along the bottom of her exposed sole, stinging. But it doesn't matter. They are close now, and only one thing matters.

The boathouse is larger than she imagined, a square-shaped stone dwelling with a thatched roof, parts of which have been torn off entirely. Two shuttered windows are carved into the front side of the house on either side of a small wooden door. An old rusted spade leans against the side of the house, a small water pump in the otherwise barren front yard. The place looks abandoned.

Vänna leads Amir across the yard and into the boathouse. The door is unlocked and gives with a small, bitter squeak. Inside there's no light but that coming in through the gaps in the rooftop, and it takes a few seconds after they enter for the children's eyes to adjust to the darkness. They see the mostly empty interior—only a half-dozen flat tables of pale plywood, a sink and counter fit for gutting fish.

Vänna looks out the north-facing window. A wooden staircase outside switchbacks down the cliff to a small, narrow dock. This is the place. In a couple of hours, maybe sooner, the ferryman will come.

"Let's go wait down there," Vänna says. "We'll stay by the cliffside."

She takes Amir's hand and leads him back out the door, but before they reach it, Colonel Kethros and his soldiers walk in.

They turn and run to the window, but the soldiers reach them and pull them back inside.

Vänna pushes them away. She takes Amir close to her, crosses her arms around his chest. She stares at the colonel.

"Why are you doing this?" she asks. "What difference does it make to you?"

The colonel sighs. He pulls a wooden chair from below the counter and carries it over to where the children stand. He sets it down a couple of feet from them and he sits. He wipes the sweat from his brow and then slowly, meticulously, unlaces his left boot and rolls up his pant leg over his caramel-colored prosthesis. He undoes the straps that hold the limb to his knee. As the false leg comes loose, a ring of red gashed flesh is visible on the underside of the colonel's skin. It leaks blood, fresh and mingling with the ridges of his amputation scar. The colonel sits back, airing his wound.

"What difference does it make to *you*?" he asks.

The colonel waves over Elias and Alexander. He points at Vänna.

"Take her, and then come back for us," he says, then turns to Amir. "I'd like some time alone with this one."

"Take her to the staging area?" Alexander asks.

The colonel shakes his head. "No, no, take her home," he says. "Let her mother deal with her."

The soldiers move in and take Vänna by the arm, and it is only then that the small boy whom they've exerted so much effort chasing at their superior's behest, the boy who until now appeared so small and terrified in the way he stared at the colonel that they'd almost forgotten about him completely, comes alive in rage. As soon as they take Vänna by the arm, he lets out a scream and begins clawing and kicking at them with such violence, they are momentarily forced backward. One of the brothers takes Vänna in a bear hug and the other does the same with Amir, and in this way they are able to keep them apart, but neither will let up until Kethros reattaches his prosthesis and stands and grabs the little boy and tosses him clean off his feet and onto the ground.

"Enough," the colonel says, and the room grows quiet.

He moves in Vänna's direction. She does not recoil, instead leaning forward to meet him, teeth bared. He removes her dislodged slipper from his pocket, kneels down, and slides it gently back on her foot. Then he rises.

"Go on," he says to his soldiers. "Take her home, then come back."

"You're a coward," Vänna says as the soldiers drag her away.

"We're all cowards," the colonel replies. "The world is a coward."

The soldiers pull Vänna out of the boathouse and around back to where their truck is waiting. At first she kicks at them, and even though they are twice her size and both they and she know it is a useless thing, the kicking reminds the soldiers of previous times they've been attacked this way. In the past it was the migrants—angry, disoriented, foreigners who tried to fight them off outside the gates of the detention center. Foreigners who screamed for the spouses and children from whom they'd been separated, and in the primal rage of their screaming could be dismissed as barbaric, undeserving of civility. In those previous instances the brothers responded with violence, hurt these aliens instinctually, the way one swats at a burrowing mosquito and, if he hits his own limb in the process, so be it.

But they respond with no such violence this time, not only because of the age and gender of their captive, but because, like all soldiers, they maintain a subconscious ledger of who they are free to hurt and who they are obliged to protect, and if they are not to protect a girl such as this one—a girl born into this place and this language and this skin—they protect no one at all. The soldiers drag Vänna to the waiting truck and force her into the back and the whole time neither of them will look her in the eye.

Chapter Twenty-eight

Before

I n the last moments some held on dearly, leaving splinters of nail and streaks of blood between the boards. And although earlier the boat was filled with screaming, of these remaining few none made a sound. Others, knowing now what was about to happen, what was inevitable, gave in, and without resistance were swept off the deck and into the water. And they, too, made no sound.

In the distance the island, the colored lights, the music.

One final time the waves lifted the *Calypso* high. Under the force of a tumbling body, the mast snapped at its base. The sea overwhelmed, drowning the bloom of limbs that struggled to escape the lower quarters. Turning past the point of rebound, the old fishing boat flung its last few occupants still hanging on to the far starboard side into the air. For an instant the deck became perpendicular to the surface of the water and then, like a closing eyelid, met it.

Amir took flight. Headlong into the seaborne sky, the roof of the great inverted world. In meeting him the water was not cold or concussive but warm and tranquil, its temperature the temperature of a body, the temperature of blood. With ease and without pain, he flew past the surface, past the depths, past the places where light and life surrendered and the domain of stillness began. And then lower, farther, past the crust of a million interlocking bodies who'd braved this passage before him and come to rest at the bottom, sick with the secrets of their own unallowed mourning. Past the smallest flour-white bones, past the world at the feet of the world. To the lowest deep, then a lower deep still. Until finally to a dry womb of a place in which were kept safe and unchanging everyone he had ever known, and everyone each of those had ever known, outward forever to encompass the whole of the living and the lived. And each of these the boy met, in their old lives and their new lives waiting, and from each drew confession and each he felt into as though there were no barrier between them, no silo of self to keep a soul waiting. What beautiful rebellion, to feel into another, to feel anything at all.

And then he surfaced.

Chapter Twenty-nine

After

Not long after it leaves the boathouse, the military truck comes to a stop. Vänna sits in the windowless back, unsure of why they aren't moving, only certain that they haven't been driving long enough to reach their destination. On the wooden bench across from her, in this vehicle that has only ever been used to transport soldiers and prisoners, Elias sits with his head down, his gaze focused intently on Vänna's feet.

The truck idles for a while, then the engine goes dead. Elias taps on the small sliding plate in the steel divider that separates the cab from the back. His brother slides the plate open.

"What's the problem?" Elias asks.

"Goats," Alexander replies.

"What?"

"Goats, goats. What do you want me to do?"

The brothers give each a pair of accusative shrugs, the universal means by which two men simultaneously abdicate responsibility for something over which they have had no control in the first place.

"Stay here," Elias says to Vänna. He gets up and unlocks the back doors. In the moment between when they swing open and when the soldier hops out and locks them shut again, Vänna catches a glimpse of where they've stopped. It's the narrowest stretch of land on this corner of the island, a place where the road slims down to a single lane in each direction over a land bridge about fifty feet above the sea. Were it not for this sliver, the two parcels of land that make up the northeast end of the island would be islands themselves.

As soon as the doors close, Vänna stands up and peers through the still-open metal grate. Out the front window she sees the brothers arguing with an old shepherd. Behind them, a small herd of snowshoe goats meanders in no particular direction, singing. It's a breed native to the central mountains, its name derived from the animals' flat, wide hooves. Vänna watches the shepherd and the brothers as they each point to the goats with great intensity, as though someone involved in the conversation had not yet become aware of the animals' existence. The three men yell. The goats sing.

In a way she enjoys the absurdity of it, the way the absurdity grates on the nerves of these two young men who have been told their entire adult lives with great, solemn seriousness that theirs is the most consequential profession, the one so central to the keeping of evil from good that it requires its own parallel morality. To see men like that, their rifles slung limply over their shoul-

ders, trying in vain to shoo away a herd of serene, singing goats, offers a small vent for her hatred. She wishes
nothing else on these two soldiers but to spend the rest
of their military lives doing exactly this.

For ten minutes the soldiers and the shepherd wrangle
the animals, until finally all are off the road and ambling
uphill, away from the end of the bridge and the shoreline.
Sweating and aggravated, Elias and Alexander walk back
to the waiting truck.

Vänna retreats from her lookout by the small metal
window. She sits down on the floor, close to the rear
doors. She kicks off her sandals and presses her knees
close to her chest. She waits.

Elias walks around the back of the truck and swings
the doors open. A pair of feet meet him, the force knocking him to the ground. Before he realizes what's happening, Vänna is out and running.

Elias yells at her to stop and then yells at his brother
for help, and quickly both Elias and Alexander are chasing Vänna. They close the gap and almost catch up with
her when she jumps onto the stone barrier at the edge of
the bridge. She stands there facing the soldiers, who stop
dead in their tracks and raise their hands at her, pleading.

"Hold on, hold on," Elias says. "It's fine—you can go
home on your own if you like, just come down from
there."

Behind and below her Vänna hears the sound of the
waves. She imagines waves sound the same everywhere,
this hush-swoop-hush, this tumbling respiration. The
soldiers approach, inching forward, their arms outstretched toward her.

"Don't," says Alexander. "Everything's going to be all right, just don't."

Vänna raises herself onto the balls of her feet. She lifts her arms up and outward and feels the breeze between her fingers. She leans back. The bridge turns to sky, the ground to air.

How beautiful in their simplicity are the constituent parts of flight. This magic of endless falling that wraps itself around her, this way the body becomes a lightness and the lightness a world. It requires no trajectory, no destination, only a parcel of air and the willingness to never land.

In the boathouse at the end of the island Amir and the colonel are alone. The boy, shuffling back in self-defense, stares wild-eyed at the officer.

He looks the part, this brick of a man who is his hunter. In the old country all the soldiers Amir ever saw were either scrawny juveniles or plump and middle-aged. But this man—trim, broad, possessed of a physical dignity—looks the way soldiers look in the movies. Were this another life Amir might have observed the colonel not with abject fear but with awe, with admiration.

Kethros paces the room, unhurried, unconcerned, as though the boy weren't there at all. He runs his finger along one of the empty plywood tables, clearing a thin trail in the years-long accumulation of dust, his finger and the table making a whispering sound. He pulls on one of the meat hooks drilled into a nearby ceiling beam, the wood squealing under the weight. He breathes in the stale mothball air.

And then he speaks, and when he does, the foreign language Amir expects to come from his lips is instead a perfect, flawless Arabic—not the stilted phonetics of foreigners who've learned from textbooks, not even the distant dialect of a different Arab country, but the exact accent of Amir's country, his city, his people.

"I know this place," the colonel says.

He sits down on a wooden chair, its reed-thatched back fraying. He takes off his military beret and tosses it on a nearby counter and not once does he acknowledge Amir, who huddles in the far corner of the room, not once does he look in the boy's direction. Instead he studies the empty plywood tables.

"We had a shipwreck here, when I was very young," he says. "It was a fishing boat, it got caught out in a bad storm. It was a charity run—that means they were out catching fish for the monks up in the monasteries. Back then you were expected to do that at least once a month, alms of a sort. That's why up to the mountain they've chiseled each of the fishermen's names onto the side of a huge cloudstone plaque. No one reads them, but they're there.

"I remember the bodies started washing up on the shore and the municipality brought them here first. They were laid out side by side, maybe on these same tables. It was an ugly thing to see, all of them together like that. The dead deserve their space. But they had to put them somewhere until they could put them in the ground. I know you people bury your dead quickly. Maybe you're afraid of them, or maybe they're afraid of you. Here we take a little more time, a little more care.

"We had an old man running the coroner's office on the island back then, this British doctor who got his start sawing off limbs in the First World War and was pretty well deaf and blind by the time he got here. They brought him out to this boathouse, this makeshift morgue they'd set up, to play supervisor. We've always been good at that, deferring to these foreigners from the mainland.

"This old man arrives, and what's the first thing he does? He says he needs a dozen rolls of twine and twenty little bells, one for each of the dead. Everyone thinks that he's gone crazy, but he's supposed to know, so they do what he says. And when they bring him these things, he takes the twine and wraps one end around the big toe of the first corpse, then runs it to the next, and the next and the next, hanging a little bell on each line. Until he's built this jangling spiderweb that connects all the corpses. Finally one of the medics works up the nerve to ask him why he's done this, and the old man says it's in case any of the sailors aren't really dead. If one of them should move, he says, the bells will ring, and we'll know right away.

"I remember when my father told me that story, it made me so angry. Here's this man who's supposed to be a doctor, a learned man, whatever that means, and he's worried about make-believe, he's worried about ghosts."

Kethros stands up. He leans against the plywood table. He flicks a sliver of sawdust; it hangs for a moment in the air.

"But that's what I do now," the colonel says. "That's what I've been reduced to, chasing ghosts."

He approaches Amir, who backs away until he's up against the room's far wall. The colonel kneels down and brushes a black curl away from Amir's eye. He opens the small bell-shaped locket around the boy's neck, and looks from the faces within to the boy's own face.

"What's your name?" he asks.

"Amir."

"Amir, Amir," the colonel repeats. "Amir of the believers, Amir of the apostles. Tell me, was that girl kind to you?"

"Yes."

"Of course she was," the colonel says. "They all are. And what do you think the prerequisite for kindness is? Have you ever tried to be kind to someone better off than you?"

Amir says nothing. In this closeness he can see the sweat beading on the colonel's forehead, the tiny pouches of fat beneath his eyes, the silvering hairs along his temples, and each tiny detail, in its evidence of mortality, of hurrying age, scrapes away at the veneer of soldiering physique he observed from a distance.

"Don't worry," the colonel says, patting the boy on the cheek. "I'm not your accuser. I don't care what you are."

Kethros lifts himself back up, wincing as his knee unbends. At a nearby sink he washes the dust off his hands. A distant rumbling sound comes in through the open windows, mingling with the sound of the sea.

"But *you* should know what you are," he says. "You are the temporary object of their fraudulent outrage, their fraudulent grief. They will march the streets on your behalf, they will write to politicians on your behalf, they will cry on your behalf, but you are to them in the end nothing but a hook on which to hang the best possible image of themselves. Today you are the only boy in the world and tomorrow it will be as though you never existed."

Amir eyes the cabin's front door, wide open, the cliffside and the forest visible just a few hundred feet away.

"Hate me all you want, but at least to me you exist," the colonel says. "To me you've never stopped existing."

Amir springs up. He runs for the door. He makes it halfway across the room before he feels the neck of his shirt pulled back to choke him, the stopping force so great he is for a second lifted clean off his feet.

"No," the colonel says. He drags Amir backward, grips him by the neck, pushes him against the back wall. "No more."

Amir screams. He kicks at the colonel, he thrashes and claws, but is easily subdued.

"I'm going to take you back to the camp, where you'll be fingerprinted and entered into the system," the colonel says, unaware of the shadow building in the doorway behind him. "We will do this properly, like civilized people. We will have good form."

The colonel feels a small displacement of air, a gray sliver moving in the farthest periphery of his vision, and upon turning is too late to defend himself against the spade that collides with the side of his head.

Colonel Kethros falls, his grip on Amir coming loose. On the ground, unmoving, he reveals to the boy the sight of Vänna Hermes, soaked and bloodied, a gash open across her left cheek. She tosses the spade on the ground.

"*Yallah*, Zaytoon," she says.

They race hand in hand down the cliffside staircase that leads from the boathouse to the dock. There's no time; one way or another, the soldiers will come for them again. The island is too small—there's no life to be had here. They don't stop running until they reach the final piling where an unmarked powerboat is anchored. An old man climbs down from the bridge. He inspects them both, frowning.

"Where will you take him?" Vänna says, and upon hearing her flawless command of the language, the ferryman remembers what Madame El Ward told him—he is to take only one migrant; the girl is not a foreigner.

"There's a community near the port," he says. "His people, they take care of their own. Do you know his sect, his ancestry, his hometown?"

"No," Vänna replies.

"They'll help him anyway; they're not going to turn their backs on a little boy all alone. But it's better if . . . you know."

"He's not alone," Vänna says, and before the old man can protest she is pulling on the anchoring rope, the boat sliding closer. Gently she guides Amir onto the deck, and then she follows.

"I don't do locals," the ferryman says. "I don't want trouble—we have to keep this quiet."

"I'm not local," the girl replies. "I'm not anything. Let's go—there's Ministry people who know we're here and if they catch you, I think you know how this will end."

The ferryman looks up at the cliffside. "Please," he says feebly. "He's not your problem."

"That's right," Vänna replies.

They set sail. In time the sea unparts and the mainland appears on the horizon, the roar and rumble of the ports, a floating jam of cruise ships and tankers, the city so dense its low white buildings seem to shove one another into the sea. Amir stands on the deck, the wind crisp against his skin. He stares out at the dawning metropolis, its awful bigness.

He holds his friend's hand. He waits on home.

Chapter Thirty

Now

T he sunheads whistle. A northward breeze sets the sleep-gum leaves to dancing. From upland the cliffside restaurant fills the air with the smell of charred lamb and rosemary. The hotel house band plays on the patio, songs the middle-aged tourists remember from their youth. A shipping magnate, drunk on the day of his sixtieth, tosses a Champagne flute off the edge of the cliff and buys everyone a round.

They come here for what is tranquil, what is undisturbed. They come to visit the mountainside monasteries and the ancient ruins, to hunt for a nest of copper arrowheads or a poem chiseled into stone or perhaps even the remains of the island's ancient dead themselves. They come to see time autopsied, to marvel from the safety of the present at the endlessly dying past.

But more than anything, they come for the sea. They come to bathe in the glass-clear tide and run squealing from the harmless surf and watch at sunset as the water takes on a low fire. In a way the sea makes them children again, returns them to a time when the world was an unbounded thing, made only to be immersed in, made only for joy.

A newlywed couple slip off their shoes and start a stumbling conga line; an old woman at the bar claps along. A moment later the hotel's duty manager takes the microphone from the house-band singer and informs the tourists that in another hour the beach will reopen. A cheer rises from the crowd; the day isn't lost.

• • •

The child lies on the shore. But for his smallness, he looks no different from the rest of the dead whose bodies litter the beach. A man, masked and gloved to protect himself from disease, approaches. He kicks at the boy's leg and, eliciting no response, kneels down beside him. He places his hands gently into and under the sand so as to lift the boy's head. He observes the child, the lightness of him, the bell-shaped locket he wears. Somewhere farther up the road police officers argue with soldiers over jurisdiction and photographers clamor for position and tourists gawk at the shipwrecked dead, but these people and their concerns belong to a different world, a different ordering of the world. A fantasy.

With great and delicate care, the masked man lifts the necklace from around the little boy's neck.

Acknowledgments

Anna, Anne, Sonny. First and always.

I am deeply grateful to Tim O'Connell for his generosity, and for editing this book under incredibly difficult circumstances. For reading early drafts, providing invaluable feedback and, more so, for their friendship, I also owe an immense debt to Jared Bland, Daniel Dagris and Carolyn Smart.

At Knopf Doubleday, I have had the astounding good fortune to work with some of the best minds in publishing. For their work on this novel and the previous one, I am grateful to Gabrielle Brooks, Madeleine Denman, Amy Edelman, Nicholas Latimer, Robert Shapiro, Suzanne Smith and Angie Venezia.

Over the last few years, several of my favorite writers, whose work has changed my life, have shown me more kindness than I deserve. Chief among them are Garth Greenwell and Emily St. John Mandel. My gratitude as well to Peter Heller, David Means and Elliot Ackerman for their generosity.

I am thankful to Literary Arts—one of the finest writing organizations in the world—for being a source of community and support.

This, as everything, is for my mother. And for Theresa, Dahlia and Idris—my world.

A Note About the Author

Omar El Akkad is an author and journalist. He has reported from Afghanistan, Guantánamo Bay and many other locations around the world. His work earned Canada's National Newspaper Award for Investigative Journalism and the Goff Penny Award for young journalists. His writing has appeared in *The Guardian, Le Monde, Guernica, GQ* and many other newspapers and magazines. His debut novel, *American War,* is an international best seller and has been translated into thirteen languages. It won the Pacific Northwest Booksellers' Award, the Oregon Book Award for fiction and the Kobo Emerging Writer Prize and has been nominated for more than ten other awards. It was listed as one of the best books of the year by *The New York Times, The Washington Post, GQ,* NPR and *Esquire* and was selected by the BBC as one of one hundred novels that changed our world.

A Note on the Type

This book was set in Minion, a typeface produced by the Adobe Corporation specifically for the Macintosh personal computer, and released in 1990. Designed by Robert Slimbach, Minion combines the classic characteristics of old-style faces with the full complement of weights required for modern typesetting.

Typeset by Scribe
Philadelphia, Pennsylvania

Printed and bound by LSC Communications
Harrisonburg, Virginia

Designed by Michael Collica